MW00977072

FROM DARKNESS
2 LIGHT

The Journey Ends

Alma D. Bass

Wasteland Press

Shelbyville, KY USA
www.wastelandpress.net

From Darkness 2 Light:
The Journey Ends
by Alma D. Bass

First Printing – July 2013
ISBN: 978-1-60047-883-3
Library of Congress Control Number: 2013943552

This book is a work of fiction. Any resemblance to anyone,
living or dead, is purely coincidental. If I have used a name
that is familiar, It is purely accidental. All historical
references to places and things are used in the context of the
story. Biblical Scriptures from the King James Version of the
Holy Bible. I hope you enjoy the book!! (Alma Dutch Bass I)

Printed in the U.S.A.

0   1   2   3   4   5   6   7

To the men in my life:
Crawford Bass, Carl Douglas Dutch, and David E. Taylor

Faith in God is a sovereign amelioration against tormenting fears. Many Christians have God for their strength but not him for their song; they walk in darkness: but those who have God for their strength ought to make him their song, that is, give him the glory of it, and take to themselves the comfort of it. This salvation is from the love of God the Father, it comes to us through God the son, it is applied by the new-creating power of God the Spirit which are ONE. We all are in different places theologically but when we have been brought from darkness to light; we all begin to seek the truth.

Excerpt from a sermon by:
Bishop George Dallas McKinney at
St. Steven's Cathedral GOGIC
San Diego, CA "1999"

PART I

CHAPTER ONE
"The Reunion"

It's not against the law for a man to want something that is beyond his reach or control; it's about how you handle it when it comes to you.

"What am I doing here?" July 12, 1994 Calvin Logan sat in the small folding chair and fidgeted with his tie while mopping his brow with the stark white handkerchief that he frowned at and examined to make sure there was no stain. The suit he wore was immaculate and blended perfectly with his dark brown skin and chiseled features which called into question his 55 years of life. His black hair was gray at the temples and painstakingly brushed into place. Most women took a second glance whenever he adorned a room. He knew exactly who he was and whose he was so he portrayed no lack of confidence that anyone could see. "Don't judge a book by its title. Open it and look inside," was one of his favorite maxims. After being a civilian employee for the United States Navy for the past 20 years, his thoughts had been strictly focused on retirement; but he had two years to go.

"I won't work when I'm 60." Calvin told this to anyone who'd listen. He'd spent ten years on active duty, serving in Vietnam which he struggled to forget, except for Trahn. Since the death of his wife of seven years, Diana, relationships were far from his consciousness. He still carried hurtful memories and guilty baggage from that experience and struggled to leave it all behind; that's why he found himself in the modest office interviewing for a job he didn't really want; new place, new challenges, looking around at all the photos that graced the walls, students past and present.

"I am so looking towards retirement but I have given my word to my friend Sam Smith that I would come for an interview, something I've never had to do with the position I currently hold. Evidently the woman in charge of the music department at the Georgia State Music

School for the Blind is a stickler for details and insisted that she be the one to conduct the interview.

"Oh joy." He said facetiously. After finishing Seminary he'd become a civilian Chaplin and Rehab counselor for the Navy. Now he was being asked to set up some activities for blind people which would be a challenge but totally within his capability. He thought about how he loved basketball in his youth.

"When the door to the office opened, my heart stopped beating for a second and my mind was in an uproar when I saw the woman walk into the room. I was there waiting to be interviewed as a favor to a friend. However, my thinking changed the moment I saw the face that had saturated my dreams for 30 years." He was immediately on his feet trying to decide whether to run from the room or embrace her.

He watched as she slowly folded the white cane with the red tip and placed it under her right arm. The fact that she appeared to be blind had not penetrated his mind and it really didn't matter. All he knew was that she was standing there close to him. At that moment, Calvin couldn't decide whether to slap her face or take her in his arms and never let go, ever again. "Hello, Sarah," he uttered.

Even after thirty years, his voice was instantly recognizable. "Calvin, is it really you?" Sarah Hansen said, trying to catch the breath that was stuck somewhere between her chest and lips. She couldn't believe that she was hearing his voice again. Instantly she was filled with happiness, sadness, and guilt.

"Calvin Logan...?" She stammered. Sensing where he stood and smelling his cologne, she got close to him and threw her arms around his neck and squeezed tightly. She stepped away and took his face in her hands wanting to "braille him" to see what he looked like after so many years. She needed to read his features with her hands. She began at his forehead; proceeded to his eyes, nose, and then his mouth. Her fingers touched his lips intimately which made him recoil.

"What...?" Calvin stepped back from her touch. He didn't understand what she was doing. The touch of her hand aroused him.

"Yes, Sarah it's me!" Calvin stammered. "I'll take the job."

"But you don't even know what the job entails. Don't you want to discuss the salary and what your duties will be?" Sarah asked, smiling deeply.

"No need," Calvin began. "Now that I know you'll be my boss, I might do it for free."

Calvin Logan watched Sarah Elaine Hansen, his childhood sweetheart, and the woman he was supposed to marry, maneuver around the small desk that filled most of the room and marveled at how well she found her way to the chair. He listened in awe as she explained the details of what the Georgia State Music School for the Blind was looking for in their new employee. He wished that her still beautiful gray eyes were not covered with dark glasses that threatened to fall off her nose anytime and she could see what he was feeling, but he was glad that she couldn't see the tears of joy that stained his face. He silently thanked and cursed God for bringing him to this place. She looked so perfectly normal that he took his hand and ran it across her face and eyes to see if there would be a reaction. There was none!

"How could she be blind?" The question rolled around in his mind and he lost total concentration on what she was saying.

"How does that salary sound to you, Calvin?" Sarah said, catching him off guard and deep in thought. As he listened to her melodic voice, he felt a stirring in his loins. Happy to be seated, he took the hat he held in his hand and placed it strategically on his lap. This only happened when he was in her presence. These emotions were never this strong; even with his deceased wife, Diana, with whom he spent seven years of his life before her tragic demise. Diana needed one last drink and it had cost her everything, including her life. A touch of sadness crossed his psyche and brought him back to reality.

"Calvin?"

"I'm sorry, Sarah, what were you saying?"

"I was asking if the salary was acceptable," Sarah replied. "I'm sure $60,000 a year is an insult but that's all we can offer at this time."

"Oh, of course," he replied. "I have a pension coming in the future and I think your offer will tide me over until then. Besides, Sam is a friend."

Abruptly and without much thought she said, "Calvin, I'm so sorry for how I treated you back..."

"Stop," Calvin said, "no need to apologize. It's all water under the bridge." He gritted his teeth, clinched his jaw and said, "Can we go someplace and talk."

"Yes," Sarah smiled. "Follow me."

Calvin watched as Sarah retrieved the white cane, moved away from her desk, went directly to the exit door, and started walking down the hallway towards another part of the building.

Not sensing him beside her, suddenly she stopped and looked back to where Calvin should have been standing and asked, "You coming?"

"How did you do that? How did you know I was not beside you or in front of you? You're amazing." Calvin whispered.

"Oh, I can feel you!" Sarah said, laughing heartily with a touch of innuendo.

She led him to her favorite place in the whole school. It was called "Sarah's Place". Sarah had begun this special program for the entire class of blind people that attended this specialized facility. The students attended the school to learn to read and play music, as well as sing. However, Sarah always felt they needed more. So she had taken some of the money left to her by her wealthy deceased husband, James Hansen, and commissioned this sanctuary-recreation room. She only wanted to remember the good things about James, which was a challenge. That's why they were hiring the Reverend Calvin Logan. This place was to be an area where the students could come and just play. The large room was equipped with recreational things like, "Beep" balls, large print and braille playing cards, braille bingo cards, dominoes and checkers and a whole wall filled with the books of the Bible transcribed in Braille.

Sarah Hansen had been the first blind music teacher hired by the school located in Albany, Georgia and was proving to be invaluable to them. After leaving James and returning home to Newport Tennessee, the then blind Sarah had returned to college and received her Master's Degree in music, majoring in choral singing through the Disabled Student's Department. Her reputation for excellency was wide spread in rehabilitation circles.

Off to one side of the huge room was another area that had a large cross hanging over the entry door. It was a chapel. It was furnished with chairs and a huge podium which held a Braille version of the Psalms. On the wall was some writing that said, "Jesus luv's y'all and so duz I."

Thinking that maybe she didn't know, Calvin told Sarah, "That saying on the wall is very nice but it's misspelled."

"No, it's not," Sarah replied. "That's what my Grandmother Maggie always told me when I was a child and that is just how she said it so I want to leave it that way as a tribute."

"I remember," Calvin whispered.

"Would you like some coffee?" Sarah asked.

"Now how is she going to accomplish that?" Calvin thought, but he said, "Yes, very much." He was beginning to believe that there was not too much she couldn't do. He watched and followed her back into the great room where he observed a table sitting over against one wall that held a small coffee pot with all the fixings for two cups of coffee. He watched fascinated as she prepared the coffee maker with coffee and retrieved two Styrofoam cups. She then went to a small sink and filled the coffee pot with water, sticking her index finger into the pot so that she could feel when it was full. After the coffee perked and was to her satisfaction, she turned to Calvin and said, "How do you take it, cream, and sugar?" He was astonished. He swallowed hard to push down the anger that formed in his throat. "If only!"

Seated at one of the long tables located in the middle of the room, they began to talk. They shared all of the years they had been apart. Sarah told Calvin about the time she spent married to James Hansen Jr., the man who had dominated and shaped her life for 30 years. She told him the good, the bad and the ugly. She left nothing out. She shared the secret that had been kept for 26 years, which was; she had given up a child, a daughter, born out of wedlock. How she had searched for and eventually found her Rebecca. She even spoke the name she had vowed never to mention again, Mr. Lawrence, her daughter's father whom she never really got to know because he was her high school music teacher. Calvin had always been her best friend so she had no misgivings about sharing her story. She had no idea of the hurt and pain she was causing him with every mention of James' and her life together. Of course, she couldn't see his expression or anguish. She told him of the auto accident that caused her to lose her sight, all of the trauma, as well as the insight, she experienced because of it. She also shared that she was very aware that without God in her life, none of what she did now would have been possible. They talked about all the familiar things they remembered about Newport, Tennessee, where they had grown up together, their families and mutual friends. Sarah was trying desperately to ask for his forgiveness without expressing the words.

It finally became too much for Calvin and he reached across the table and took her hand into his and asked, "Why, Sarah?" He snapped as he pressed his fingers into her palms. "Why didn't you wait for me like you promised?"

"Calvin, you're hurting me," she whined, pulling her hand away. For the first time she felt frightened and unsure.

Calvin waited for her to say more, and when she didn't, he began to fill her in on his life without her. He told her of how he felt when he received her "Dear John" letter on board a Navy ship in the Port of Tonkin outside Vietnam. He made her remember how he rushed to her side when she married James and begged her to go with him, but it was too late. He was now in a rage just remembering that day. He remained silent for a while not wanting her to hear his anger. He told her of his marriage to Diana, his leaving the Navy, his call into the ministry, and then he told her about Trahn, his ward from Vietnam. His heart swelled with pride when he talked about Trahn.

"I was in Vietnam until the end of the war," he began. While on shore duty one day, I and some of my crew ran across this wounded kid of about 10 years old. Naturally we took him back to the hospital ship where we found out that he had no family that could be located. Somehow we bonded and I have been supporting him ever since. I told him that I would adopt him as soon as you and I were married." He waited for her to respond.

"Isn't he a grown man now?" Sarah asked. "Why do you still support him?"

"Long story," Calvin said, wondering the same thing. "I plan to bring him to the United States soon. I never imagined it would take so long." In his heart he also blamed Sarah for that.

Before Sarah could respond she heard the sound of tapping canes and the rattle of harnesses attached to the collars of the guide dogs some of her students utilized. She pushed the button on the talking watch she wore and discovered that she and Calvin had been talking for three hours. Calvin didn't tell her that several people had come to the door in those few hours but had not disrupted their conversation.

"I guess we should wrap this up," she said. "Do you have any questions about the things we want to do for the students here? There has been some interest shown by the students in some religious studies and, of course, sports by some of the young men. I understand that you work in this field in your current job."

"I do", Calvin said. "I work in the civilian sector but I deal with rehabilitating military men and women. You do know that I'm a minister? I think I can handle the religious part." He felt like an idiot standing there with the broad smile on his face that she couldn't see. "Well, when do I start?"

Calvin reached for her hand and shook it firmly wanting to pull her closer to him. Her skin was soft to his touch, but firm, which belied her years. She was still very beautiful to him. Her long sandy-brown hair was now cut to just below her shoulders and her light-brown skin showed very little sign of aging. He smiled when he realized that she had not grown an inch over her 5'2" frame. Her figure was still good and she smelled like a fresh summer breeze. How he'd missed the times they spent together. "Why didn't she wait?" He asked himself again. Once more he felt anger and betrayal. He knew he must overcome these feelings if he was going to work with her.

"May I help you back to your office?" He asked.

"No, I'll be fine," Sarah said. He let go of her hand.

"I can start as soon as I get back from Norfolk, Virginia." Calvin explained. "I have to go back and give a two week notice, close up my home and tie up some other loose ends."

"Welcome aboard." Sarah said. "I'm so glad you came back.....; I mean," she stammered, "I am so glad you are taking the position.

"Ditto!" He whispered as he watched her carry herself through the door and out of his sight. "WOW," he whispered.

CHAPTER TWO
"TRAHN"

Back at her desk, Sarah reached for the telephone with the raised dots of braille on them and dialed the number effortlessly. "Mama", she began, guess who was just here with me?"

"Who is that, my dear?" Sarah's mother, Suzanne Justin, responded.

"Calvin. Do you remember Calvin, Mama?"

"I think so. Ain't that the Bishop's son. What's he doing there with you and where are you? When are you coming home, Sarah?"

"Mama, is anyone there with you? Is Mable there? Put her on the phone please."

"Yes, Dear," Suzanne responded.

"Hello Sarah," Mable began. "I think you need to come home pretty quick if you wanna' see yo' Mama again. She is going down pretty fast and all she talks about is her little Sarah just like you was still a babe or something. You know I been taking care of her since you left here and she not doing so good right now. Do you hear me?"

Mable Goodlow had been a God send to Sarah when she took the job in Albany. Her mother, Suzanne, had refused to leave Newport, Tennessee and move to Albany, Georgia with her. She had told Sarah, "You go ahead, Child. Your daddy, Paul, told me that I should just stay right here so that he can keep an eye on me so he can make sure that I'm okay." Paul Justin had died in 1968 but he was still very alive to Suzanne. He was still as much a part of her life as he'd ever been. The people of Newport still talked about how that White boy had married that "colored" girl and stayed together all them years and had that pretty little girl that married that rich colored man and he made her go blind. "Shame; shame; shame!"

Suzanne was now in poor health which the doctors called "unrequited grief." Now in her late 80's, Suzanne would do anything for her daughter except leave Newport. Sarah trusted Mable to care for her and to be truthful when there was a problem. She didn't question it when Mable told her to get there, and she would.

"Ok, Mable, I'll be there as soon as possible. Take care of her, please."

"I will, Ms. Sarah, you just hurry now, you here?"

Calvin had been back in Norfolk, Virginia for a week and hadn't told her when he would return and Sarah was in a quandary as to how she was going to get to Newport. Her students had a singing commitment she needed to keep because these fundraisers were how they stayed in business. Whenever budget cuts were needed, somehow the music department was the first on the chopping block.

She was now the assistant director of the music department and the Director, Sam Smith, trusted her to make some hard decisions when it came to fund-raising. The students had garnered a good following in the years that Sarah had been in charge. Not only did they perform in theaters and halls, they also gave free concerts at nursing facilities and private parties. Affluent people were always happy to hire "those poor blind people" to entertain at some of the lavish parties to show their friends how benevolent they were. Sarah was not at all reluctant to take advantage of every opportunity that came her way. They depended on the kindness and charity of others. They didn't shy away from being someone's 'tax-write-off.'

Sarah hadn't spoken to Calvin since he left for Norfolk. When her phone rang, she was thinking of him. "Hello Boss," Calvin said. "I know it has taken me a long time to get things straight here but I promise I'll be there soon, however, there is one more thing I have to do. I have to make a trip home to Newport to see about the Bishop so I will be delayed about a week longer. Is that okay with you?"

"I have to get to Newport also," Sarah began. My mother is not doing so well and she's asking for me."

"How had you planned on traveling there?" Calvin questioned.

"Plane, train or automobile," Sarah giggled.

"Do you do that often?" Calvin asked. "How....? She'd forgotten how Calvin used to tease her unmercifully.

"There's that question again. I am very capable of traveling on my own. I'm not helpless you know." She was feeling a little angry and frustrated. She didn't like having to explain how and why she did certain things that society thought blind people couldn't and shouldn't do. Before she could respond again Calvin said, "Since I am going that way, why don't I stop by and fetch you and take you home with me?" Expecting her to refuse, Calvin was surprised when she replied, "That would be very nice if that's not too far out of your way."

"No problem at all!" Calvin smiled at the phone. After talking to Sarah, Calvin sat down and dialed the number he had for Trahn. He still called the orphanage in DaNang, Vietnam where he had left Trahn when he left the country.

"Hullo, how may I hep you?" The voice said on the other end of the line.

"Hello, Sue Yee, this is Calvin Logan. Is Trahn available today?"

"Hullo, Mr. Calveen, ah-so, Trahn is here today. Hold, p'ease I find for you. You okay? Good to talk you."

"I am fine, Sue Yee. I will hold."

"Calveen, this is Trahn. You call me on time. I ready to leave and go home. Talk to me."

"How are you Trahn? Are you ready to come to America? I think I have everything in place now for you to join me. I never dreamed it would take so long but if you're ready, so am I. I know you don't need a father now but we all need friends and I hope that we are still friends." There was a long pregnant pause on the other end of the line.

"I good," Trahn responded. "I am ready for America. When I come to you? You keep your promise."

"Very soon now. I have gotten your Visa and Passport and I am calling to ask where you want the papers sent."

"Send to Sue Yee. I get them here. Thank you, frien'."

"Alright, Trahn, I will send the papers and please call me when you receive the information and get ready to catch the plane."

"Okay, will do"

Calvin listened as the phone call was terminated.

Trahn Van Nuyen had been raised in an orphanage in DaNang but had never wanted for anything material. Calvin Logan had kept his promise made to Trahn all those years ago. Every month since 1975, Calvin had sent a check to the orphanage for Trahn's care. When Trahn was 18 years-old he left the orphanage and had become familiar with the streets of Vietnam. He had joined in with a crime syndicate that ruled most of the city. He was involved in everything from drug dealing to gambling, prostitution and everything in between. However, he still visited the orphanage once a month to pick up his money from Calvin. None of the people at the orphanage knew of his lifestyle. He was filled with lots of anger and resentment because Calvin had promised that he would bring him to America and he had not kept his word until now.

His mother and father had been killed in the war and he never knew if any of his three sisters and two brothers had survived. He remembered very clearly the day he had stepped on that land mine and nearly lost his arm. He resented Calvin for saving him to be raised in an orphanage where he had to fight to survive (and survive he did) by whatever means necessary.

When Sue Yee handed him the letter from the United States State Department, he was filled with fear and excitement. While he'd never been in prison, he was afraid that some of his activities on the streets of Vietnam had become known to the Embassy and that they wouldn't let him leave the country with a criminal past.

The man sitting across the desk from Trahn showed no signs of suspicion that he could discern. He was just asking Trahn routine questions about his life and how he came to know Calvin Logan. He told the man the story that he'd relived countless times of how Calvin had rescued him and saved his life and become his mentor for all these years.

"Mr. Logan has taken full responsibility for your care for the first year that you are in America. You must stay in constant contact with him at all times. Is that clear?"

"Clear," Trahn responded.

"Have you received your passport yet?" The man asked

"Yes,"Trahn answered.

"Then here is your Visa that is good for one year from today. Good luck in America."

Trahn reached for the hand extended to him and shook it firmly. At the moment none of this seemed real. He would wait until he was on the airplane before he celebrated but a plan was already taking shape in his mind as to what he would do in America!

CHAPTER THREE
"GOOD-BY SUZANNE"

Calvin pulled the car to the front door of "Sarah's Place" which also served as her living quarters. She didn't like these arrangements but she was weary of fighting with Sam Smith and the other staff members about her safety. It was about 6:00 A.M. on a Monday morning. She was waiting for him because as soon as the car stopped he saw her at the front door.

He watched her unfold the cane and head towards the parked car. He leaped from the car and reached and took the small travel bag she carried and opened the car door for her to enter. She walked a few paces then reached with her hand to feel where the door was located and gracefully let herself down into the front seat, folding the cane as she went.

"How did..?" Calvin began to ask.

"Oh Calvin, will you please stop asking me how I do things. I am not helpless. God gave us all five senses and I make use of the four that I have left. It's not that they are better than anyone else, it's just that I depend on them more than sighted people. What I did just now is not as remarkable as you might think. First of all, I was expecting you this morning so I was very aware when a car pulled up in front of my door. I don't usually have visitors this time of morning. You have been to the school a couple of times so I am aware of the sound of your car's motor. Each model has a distinct sound, you know? My bag has been packed since I knew I was making the trip. All of my clothes are marked with braille markers by color and item. For example, if I want to put on a gray skirt and a pink shirt, I simply feel the tags on the hangers until I find the correct tag. When someone takes me shopping for shoes and pantyhose, they simply place the correct color pantyhose in the suitable shoes and they stay there until I wear them. After I wear them, I simply wash the stockings and place them back into the shoes they came out of and there they stay until I wear them again. The only way I am mismatched is that someone does it to me on purpose or they are color blind. I've had both kinds. Are there any more questions? Is that clear?" Sarah placed her hands on her hips as if to emphasize her annoyance.

"None that I can think of right now," Calvin laughed as he closed the door to the car, went around to the driver's side, got in and proceeded to start the engine. He glanced at her longing to touch her face and kiss her cheek. "How long will this take?" He asked, knowing that she knew the answer.

"It's a good five hour drive here or there," Sarah responded. "We should be there by noon. Thank you for the lift."

"My pleasure."

They drove the first hour virtually silent. They commented every now and then on the weather, their families and things pertaining to the school. He told her that he had some ideas that he would like to implement as soon as they got back and met with all of the students. He turned on the radio and they both listened to the music and news which delayed their need to have a conversation. Soon Sarah was fast asleep and Calvin watched her as much as he could while driving.

"Why does she still affect me so?" He reached and stroked her hand.

"Wake up Sarah, we're here," Calvin said shaking her slightly. She jumped, startled, when he touched her arm.

"My goodness," she yawned, "that was quick."

She listened as Mable reached for the handle to help her out of the car and into the house.

"I'll call you tomorrow after I've seen Dad and we can discuss when we want to return to Albany, okay?" Calvin called to her.

"Good, tell Bishop 'hello' for me." Sarah yelled over her shoulder.

"How is Mama?" Sarah asked Mable. When they entered the house that Sarah had grown up in, all the familiar smells and sounds permeated her nose and her mind and a warm feeling came over her.

As they entered the bedroom, she heard Suzanne call her name from the bed where she and her father had shared so much love. "Sarah, is that you, Baby?"

"It's me, Mama," Sarah said, reaching for the bed and sitting down next to her mother. She stroked her head and face and kissed what she thought was her cheek. Actually it turned out to be her nose.

"How you doin' Mama?" Sarah asked, tears staining her face as she gripped her mother's frail slim hand. Sarah noticed that her mother had lost a tremendous amount of weight. Suzanne had never been a big woman but she had always been healthy. For the first time Sarah was thankful that she couldn't see how the ravages of time and age had taken over her mother's body. As she held her hand Suzanne began to speak in a voice barely audible. Sarah leaned forward to hear her words.

"Sarah Elaine, I am so sorry that I was not able to help you with yo' life. You were my baby and I wanted you to stay my baby. I didn't want you to grow up and leave me and yo' daddy. And when I found out what that teacha' done to you, why I was just dumb struck. When we sent you to Savanna to be with yo' uncle Ben, I thought my heart would crack wide open, but we don't know what else to do. It don't matter that he be a White man 'cause yo' daddy is white, but he don't do nothin' for you and that child you never brung home.

"It's alright Mama that was so long ago. We don't have to talk about that now." Sarah began to weep.

"Yea' we do, Child. I'm going to join your daddy soon but he done told me to let you know that we did what we thought was right. At the time we thought that Calvin done knocked you up and we was shamed that his pappy would be mad at y'all cause y'all was so young and him being a preacha' and all. I always believed that Calvin was a good boy.

"Now there was James. James was never right for you but that's what you wanted because he had them two young'uns. They were never yours even though you wanted them to be. I never thought God would shut yo' womb for good. I thought I was going to have a house full of grand babies, but He is a wise God and His will takes priority. We didn't know how to he'p you make good choices. Can you forgive us for that? All we knowed was to love ya and raise you up the best we knowed how."

"Of course I forgive you, Mama. I always knew that you and Daddy loved me; it's just that I didn't know how to love myself, but once I met the Lord, He gave me enough love to last a lifetime." Mable walked into the room when she no longer heard their voices wanting to make sure everything was okay. She then heard a car pull up in front of the house. Sarah knew it was Calvin.

"Do you have a Bible with you," she asked when she felt his hand on her shoulder.

Calvin knew right away what she wanted because she had shared the passage of Scripture her grandmother Maggie had left for her when she died. He began to read; Romans 8:38, 39 *"For I am persuaded, that neither death, nor life...can separate us from the love of God and each other...."*

As he read, Sarah felt the grip her mother had on her hand loosen. Calvin watched as Suzanne took her last breath of life and peacefully made her transition. He reached for Sarah's hand but she refused to let go of Suzanne's. She knew her mother was gone and a part of Sarah' heart left with her. Both Sarah and Calvin began to pray. There were no more tears because she knew that God was a forgiving merciful God and that He would make sure Suzanne would join Paul wherever that might be. She had been at her mother's home for one hour, just in time to have the talk they had meant to have over 40 years ago. All was well!!

CHAPTER FOUR

The Temple of The Living God Community Apostolic Church in Newport, Tennessee was filled to capacity. It was very different from the way Sarah and Calvin remembered it. One thing, however, had not changed; Bishop Noah Logan was still the pastor after 50 years of preachin'. Calvin looked at his father with pride and awe. "How did he do it?" he asked himself. Calvin had no memory of his mother who died shortly after giving life to him. That's why he had no siblings. His father never remarried and Calvin was now 55-years old.

Bishop had immediately rushed to Sarah's side when he got the call from his son that Suzanne Justin had passed on. Although she was not a member of his congregation, he remembered the relationship his son Calvin had with Sarah. "My, my", he said, scratching his head at the wonder of the things he had seen God do. He had long ago given up on ever seeing those two together but here they sat in front of him asking him to do the services for her mother.

"Of course," he began. "I wouldn't have it any other way. Ms. Suzanne was a good God-fearin' woman and we must do right by her." Calvin glanced over at Sarah to see if there was any reaction. He was getting to know when she was not pleased with something. There was none. In the last two days, there had been mostly silence between the two of them. Sarah was off someplace where Calvin couldn't go.

On the day of the service the church was filled with flowers and people, people of every hue, from dark chocolate to milky white all sitting together and mourning as one. What a change!! Calvin began to describe the scene.

"Sarah, you wouldn't believe it. Your mother's kin the Williams family and your father's kin, the Justin family are all mixed up sitting right there together side by side. Old Mr. Jones, Ms. Harris, and all those bigots are sitting right in the middle of the church where all the black people are gathered and not one is pushing and shoving. Can you believe it?" He repeated.

When Suzanne Williams, that 'fast' colored girl, married Paul Justin, a white man, in 1941, the town had been in an uproar. This had been a first for Newport. No one thought it would last so they tried to wait them out until they got over their foolishness but the couple had fooled them all. They not only stayed together but they had a child together that looked like both sides of the family so she stuck out like a sore thumb. How things had changed.

"Tell me," Sarah asked Calvin.

Calvin began to describe what he saw. "Well, first of all, your mother looks just like she is sleeping. She has on a Pink frilly dress and everything in the casket is pink. There are so many flowers on her you can hardly tell." Sarah giggled.

"The church is so much larger than when you last saw it. Daddy, I mean, Bishop had a building fund going ever since I can remember and, when I was grown, he finally collected enough to expand the sanctuary. There is now a choir loft right behind the pulpit which seats about 50 people. Everything up there is light blue, something like the sky. The choir members are in blue robes. The carpet on the floor is a darker blue and the cushions on the pews are the same color blue with some white in it. All of your family, the ones I know, is here. Your uncle Ben and his family are taking up two pews by themselves and that nice catholic lady, (as you all referred to her), is wearing a lacy scarf on her head. She is looking at Ben with the same love she had when they first married. They must have about 17 grandchildren." Sarah laughed as she pinched him on his knee.

"Well, it's the truth," he laughed, There must be 300 people here. The church is filled to capacity and some are standing. There are 10 pews in three rows and looks like this is going to be a joyous home-going because Sister Vera Mae Sassy is getting ready to shout already and the services haven't even started yet." "Glory," Sarah laughed.

"Deacon Jeremiah done brought out the prayer cloths and there are about 20 boxes of Kleenex lining the altar. The ushers have put that look on their faces that says 'We ain't going to have no mess here today. This is going to be a dignified service and we ain't going to get these white gloves dirty.' Their white uniforms are so stiff they could stand on their own." Sarah was bent over rocking with laughter.

When she heard the strains of "*Precious Lord*" she knew instantly that it was the voice of Missus Snowden, the woman who had taught her to sing, so long ago, in the "Chill'ins Choir."

"Is that thing still around her neck?" She whispered to Calvin. "Yes," Calvin said. "That fox fur stole is a lot less intimidating now and it looks like its best days are over." Sarah could just imagine what it must look like. "Stop, Calvin, you're making my stomach ache."

"Okay, okay," he said, "but you asked." Soon they were caught up in the solemn music and the many flowery words being said about her mother. The words "Colored" and "White" were not used once during the whole service. It was as though it didn't matter anymore. God had placed such a sense of peace in her heart that no tears would come. At the end, when Calvin walked her to the casket, Sarah bent over her mother's body and whispered, "Tell Daddy hello for me," and kissed Suzanne's face for the last time. She moved Calvin's arm from her waist and unfolded her cane which she held in her hands, straightened her back and proceeded to walk down the long aisle unassisted. She could hear the comments being made such as, "Look how brave she is," to, "Oh, that poor thing, don't you think somebody should help her?"

"Please God, don't let me stumble." She silently prayed as she walked back to her seat on the front row counting her steps as she moved.

CHAPTER FIVE
"TRAHN & KIM"

Only two weeks had passed but to Sarah it seemed like a month. She sat in the living room of her mother's house and listened as Mable described the furnishings and photos that occupied the room where they were. Mable had packed all of Suzanne's personal belongings that Sarah would take with her and thanked Sarah for letting her remain in the house that had been her home for the past years. Sarah had agreed not to sell the house right away and agreed to let Mable rent it and stay there for as long as she liked.

"Mama would want that," she said. "I can't stay here in Newport because I love my job and there is nothing more left here for me. Later, much later, I'll decide what to do. Just take care of it for me."

"I surely will," Ms. Sarah.

She and Calvin were leaving to return to Albany and she anxiously awaited the sound of his car. Their boss, Sam Smith, had told them both to take all the time they needed, and not to rush back, but Sarah was very anxious to return to her students. Here she felt very lonely but Calvin kept assuring her that she was never alone.

They returned to Albany, he to his new apartment, she to "Sarah's Place" where their working relationship took on a form of normalcy. He continued to watch and marvel at how well she had adjusted to life without sight and without him.

Calvin implemented some programs that excited both Sam and the students. He even found a way to teach blind men to play basketball and golf and the women to knit and crochet. It was hard for the students to leave when their music lessons and rehearsals were over. The balls Calvin supplied made a sound when they were moved so that the men could follow where they were. They made a chirping sound, thus the name, "Beep Balls." He formed two teams and there was a competitive game every Saturday. The school was now filled with the sounds of Guide Dogs, tape recorders, tapping canes and Beep Balls. Of course the men used this for an advantage. They would place a "beep ball" in a part of the room where they wanted to rendezvous and tell a young lady they were interested in to just "follow the sound" for a clandestine meeting.

One day Sarah sat at her desk when she heard her door being flung open. It frightened her at first until she heard the excitement in Calvin's voice.

"He's here," Calvin said excitedly.

"Who's here," Sarah asked.

"Trahn, my son, ahh my friend, Trahn Van Nuyen. He's finally here. Come", he said, "Come and meet Sarah."

The moment he took her hand, Sarah almost recoiled. She felt straightaway that he was trouble. She had this uncanny ability to distinguish when there was danger or when something was amiss. Instead, she took his hand and said, "It's good to finally meet you. I've heard so much about you. Welcome to America!"

"Don't believe a word he said," Trahn said, taking the back of her hand and raising it to his lips where he gently kissed it.

"I won't," Sarah said, barely above a whisper. Her body shivered.

Sarah could hear the joy and excitement in Calvin's voice so she kept her feelings about Trahn to herself not fully understanding why she had an instant distrust and dislike for this young man. Was it jealously or something more sinister?

"We'll pick you up after work and go out to dinner this evening so you two can get to know each other," Calvin said. "You might be spending lots of time together." Sarah wondered what he meant by that statement. She had no intentions of spending any time with him. She wondered if Calvin was going to get him a job in his department working with the students or something more. She let the moment pass.

Calvin and Trahn left the school and returned to the apartment they were to share. He noticed how little belongings Trahn had brought with him. He would soon remedy that.

"You know this next year we're going to have to stay pretty close to each other and I expect you to find a job and become a trustworthy citizen."

Trahn listened and said, "Yea, you just get me a car and I'll take care of the rest. I'm good with my hands and once I learn these streets...Err, I mean the city, I'll do just fine. Maybe I could work with you until I can find something to do. What do you think?"

"That might be an idea," Calvin replied. "We'll consult Sam and I'll see what Sarah thinks about it. Right now, get unpacked so we can pick her up for dinner."

The students soon became infatuated with Trahn, especially the females. There was Anna, Leslie, LaTia, Mary, Robert, Andrew, David and Mark. These were Sarah's charges, her chosen eight. They made up the choir that toured the city, and neighboring states for the fund-raising required. Trahn wanted no part of the "religious" stuff so he only helped with the recreational duties.

Trahn was very handsome with slick black hair that was combed straight back and was bound in a pony-tail. He was 5'9" tall and very slim. His coloring was like caramel, and his accented voice was smooth and menacing, forbidding and threatening. When he asked or told the students what they should be doing, somehow they knew to do it right away.

He saw Anna walking with her cane down the hall of the school heading toward the music room. "Hello, Anna," Trahn whispered, leaning close to her ear. She jumped, startled, because she hadn't heard him approach.

"You look very pretty today and you smell so good. Can I take you out somewhere?" He continued, placing his arm around her waist.

"You want to take me out?" the twenty-year old blushed, unaware that he had his hand deep inside her purse where he removed the wallet and took out what cash was there. He continued whispering in her ear and kissed her slightly on the back of her neck which made her body shiver.

When he returned the wallet to her purse, he released his hold, smiled to himself and said, "I'll see you later. Watch your step."

Anna immediately made her way to Sarah's office and knocked; hoping to find her there. "Come in," Sarah called out.

"Ms. Hansen," Anna said. "Do you have a moment? I really need to talk with you."

"Of course, Anna." Sarah loved the fragrance Anna wore so there was no problem identifying who she was. "Is there something wrong?"

"No, I don't think so," Anna responded. "It's just that I think Trahn likes me and he has asked me out. I want to know what you think about that."

Sarah felt her hands tremble. She wanted very much to dissuade the girl from accepting this invitation but she had to be careful how she responded. The students came here to learn independence and self-reliance. Anna was 20-years old and was well able to make her own decisions but, because of Sarah's unexplained dislike for Trahn, she didn't want her to get involved with him.

"Anna, there is an unwritten rule around here that frowns upon students dating staff, however, what you do on your own time is up to you. We don't know that much about Trahn so I would suggest you get to know him better before you make any sort of commitment to him. I know that he is Mr. Logan's... (His what?) protege but you still should be cautious."

"But, he's so kind to me. Whenever he's around he's always offering to help. He tells me I am pretty and that he likes me. I can't think of any reason I shouldn't see him outside of school. My mother seems to like him too, so I'm going to think about it."

"Alright, Anna, but please be cautious." Sarah sighed.

Soon after, Sam got a report that Leslie, one of the other students, was missing some money from her purse, then another and another. He knew that they were not just making these things up because they were given a course on managing and spending money when they were enrolled in the school since most of them received benefits from the government because of their disability. They were taught to fold the paper money in a certain way depending on the denomination, for example, a single dollar bill was left unfolded while a twenty dollar bill was folded in half, etc. They were taught that a nickel had a smooth edge and a dime had a corded edge, etc. So when the students began complaining, he knew to be vigilant. "Who could be doing this?" He asked Sarah one day at a meeting. "And what can we do to combat such behavior?" Sarah immediately thought of Trahn but was reluctant to say his name without adequate proof. There was no other person that could be responsible. Besides Sarah and Calvin, the only other people to enter the building were tradesmen and care givers. The rest of the staff had no access to her students. It just didn't add up!

"I'm speaking to you in confidence, but I would keep an eye on Trahn. There is something about him that seems to rub me the wrong way. While I can't put my finger on it, I trust what I feel about people. It has not failed me so far. Don't discuss this with Calvin please. I'll handle that if necessary." Sarah explained to Sam.

From that time on there was always tension in the air whenever Trahn was around. The amount Trahn was removing from the blind student's purses and wallets was so small that Sam was reluctant to believe that he could be doing this. After all, he was receiving a salary from Calvin and he didn't understand what a few dollars more could mean to him; but he would be vigilant.

Trahn soon found his way to the streets of Albany, the seedy side. There was a small tight knit, close, Vietnamese community that was thriving. There was a certain diversified unification. It had its own shopping areas and its own brand of crime. Many different dialects of Mandarin were spoken along with different aspects of dress. This suited Trahn perfectly.

Right in the heart of the neighborhood was the Vietnamese Resource Center, funded by the US Government for the betterment of the Vietnamese immigrants who found themselves in Albany after the war. The center was operated by Pho Lý and his wife Kim. Their jobs were to identify new immigrants and make sure they had the financial and social means available to survive here in the states. They were funded generously by the United States, whether out of benevolence or guilt, the money flowed freely. They remembered the TET offensive.

The Center operated in peace by the largess of the street gangs that prayed on business owners and others, and made a monthly visit to the Center for a payment for protection.

Trahn's job was to make sure that all payments were made in a timely fashion by whatever means necessary. So far he had not had to use any real violence; just intimidation and fear. He was good at that, having had so much fear in his own life. He was always afraid that his life in America wouldn't and couldn't last despite the assurances from Calvin. He needed to acquire as much money as possible so he could, like in Vietnam, pay his way out of any situation he found himself in. Self-preservation was vital at this point. He never wanted to return to the life he had, at all cost.

One day, Trahn walked into one of his favorite restaurants and saw this woman sitting alone at a table. As he approached, Kim Lý looked up observing the handsome man walking towards her. She couldn't place the face. Kim was a very ordinary looking woman, dressed very modestly in cultural pajamas and robe worn by women of Vietnam. To Trahn, however, she was a vision of loveliness. She reminded him of the girls he had left behind. He tried to block the memory.

"May I join you?" Trahn said.

"Why would you want to do that?" Kim asked

"Because I think you were sitting here waiting for me," Trahn said, with a sly smile.

"Well, you would be wrong." Kim snapped. "I am waiting for my husband to join me and obviously you don't know who I am."

"No, but I would sure like to."

"My name is Kim Lý and my husband is Pho. Do you know him?"

"I do know him." Trahn replied not believing his good fortune. He had visited the resource center on one of his collection runs and had wondered how he could get involved with it. He had no idea what lay in store for him. He felt that if he could win over Kim, he could get what he wanted. Immediately he devised a plan that would bring him close to Kim.

Simultaneously, Kim saw in him an answer to her prayer. She had been looking for a young man just like him to complete her plot to steal more money from the center. Since she was the bookkeeper, treasurer and secretary for the center, she had full access to all of the funds provided by the U.S. government. Pho trusted her completely and had no reason to suspect that his wife was not totally loyal to what they were doing for their people. Kim had grown weary of setting up dummy accounts for Vietnamese families that didn't exist. Her scheme operated like this. She would set up an account for a non-existent family that had just immigrated to the United States, provide them with resources to get a start, which consisted of money. She would write a check to an account that belonged to her. She had stashed away a fortune but she wanted more. These people were not required to report in person, they just needed a paper trail and she supplied that. On the outside things appeared totally normal and Pho was unaware of his wife's plot

Her instincts told her that Trahn had come from the streets of Vietnam and that there was some larceny in his heart. After standing in front of her table for a moment or so, Trahn noticed that her husband had not arrived as she said so he boldly sat down across from her. She looked at him and smiled. "Do you need a job?" Kim felt a chill of excitement run down her spine.

"Shall we talk about it?" Trahn replied. Immediately a bond was formed and Trahn was in love. Soon he was spending all of his free time away from the school with Kim. They boldly met at a hotel located a short distance from the Center. Their planning and lovemaking was frantic; fulfilling long pent up desires.

The day Trahn walked into the office of the resource center to meet with Pho the palms of his hands were dripping with perspiration as he shook the man's hand. "You must be Trahn," Pho Lý said. He was wondering if Pho would recognize him from his other visits but apparently not. "I have heard good things about you. I understand you are seeking employment with us, is that correct? My wife seems to have a lot of confidence in you. How long have you been in this country?"

"Less than one year," Trahn replied, "but I have met a lot of people from our country that need help. If you hire me, I will bring these people to you so that you can serve them. I have lots of experience with needy people. I was hurt in the war and raised in an orphanage. Had it not been for my benefactor I would still be there." Pho noticed the deformity in Trahn's left arm. "I'll be an asset to you."

"Well, my wife seems to have confidence in you." He reached for Trah's right hand and said, "Welcome aboard. I'll leave you in my wife's hands and she will tell you what she wants from you."

Trahn and Kim glanced at each other with a telling look, suppressing the desire to be intimate. So a deceitful partnership was formed that soon gave him a name and reputation in Albany. "Only in America!" Trahn reflected. No more money was missing from the school and soon the incidents were forgotten to all except Sarah.

CHAPTER SIX
"REBECCA"

Sarah and Calvin were so busy with their work, at the school and getting acquainted again, that one year flew by without their noticing it. They had both fallen deeply in love with each other and could hardly keep their hands from caressing and fondling every time they were together, which was every day.

"Whenever he touches me the way he does, and strokes my bottom lip with his finger, my heart races, my knees go weak and I just want to get close to him and fall into his arms and rub my face against his chest. When he strokes my hair and whispers in my ear, my body reacts and my desire for him renders me helpless. I can just imagine myself under his body feeling the pressure of his weight, smelling that wonderful cologne he wears. It's intoxicating!" She shook herself from her reverie.

Sarah's choir was often called away for performances and they traveled extensively. Anna had become the featured lead singer, with an extraordinary voice, so they had formed a special bond. However, Sarah noticed that Anna no longer showed the same enthusiasm for traveling or singing now that she was involved with Trahn. He'd somehow lowered her confidence to where she felt she needed to be with him at all times; but it was against the rules for the school to pay for anyone other than the students to travel. So inevitably she had missed some performances.

Choir activities were not mandatory for her enrollment because this facility, Sarah's Place, was for recreation. All of the students had finished high school and some college so their participation was strictly on a volunteer basis. Anna's mother hadn't complained to the school about her relationship with Trahn because it took some of the pressure off her for Anna's care and safety. Little did she know that she had sealed her daughter's fate. Therefore, Anna's blindness had kept her at home with her family.

Calvin walked into Sarah's office, sat before her and said, "Don't you think we should get married now?" It was not unexpected but she had wanted a one-knee proposal with all the trimmings. This announcement (or question) reminded her of James; everything "matter-of-fact" no formality.

"We are not getting any younger and I want to spend the rest of my life with you," Calvin stated. "What do you think about that?" He asked. "I know this is not what you expected but, If I don't quench my desire for you, I am going to explode and ravish you right here on your desk and that would not be a good thing to do. I love you, Sarah, and I need you. My body needs you, my mind needs you and my spirit needs you; my body won't wait much longer." He reached for her hand, pulled her around the desk and whispered in her ear, "Can I have you?"

Sarah's body shivered at his touch and she grabbed his shirt to keep from falling. The tension in the room was so thick she could hardly breath.

There was no hesitation, no coyness, no apprehension whatsoever on Sarah's part. This is what she had wanted since their reunion. "Yes, Calvin, I think we should get married now." She walked from behind her desk and found his open arms. The White cane lay on the floor by her desk. Her heart guided her way to where he stood.

When she heard the door to the office close she immediately picked up the phone and pushed the braille buttons.

Rebecca St. John, Circuit Judge for the State of Michigan, looked at the number that popped up on the screen of the phone that adorned her huge mahogany desk located in her plush office. She hesitated before she picked up the receiver. She had asked her mother not to call her at work so she supposed this had to be something important.

"Hello, Mother", she said. "Are you alright? This is my work number. I'm a little busy right now."

"I know," Sarah responded, but I needed to share some news with you and it couldn't wait. Are you sitting down?"

"Yes, I am!" She snapped.

"Guess what?" Sarah said.

"Mother," Rebecca said showing some irritation, "I don't have time for guessing games. Please tell me your news."

Sarah heard the edginess in her voice and simply said, "Calvin and I are getting married." She waited for her daughter to respond. "What do you think?" she asked. "At my age…" she noticed that Rebecca had not said a word. "Dear? I want you to be my Matron of Honor and help me…."

As she contemplated her mother's question, Rebecca's mind was deep in thought. She loved her mother deeply but her new husband had not yet met that side of her family. He had met and liked her adopted White mother and father but she had delayed telling him about her "birth" mother or the fact that she was half-black, a Mulatto, a half-breed. She lived in a mostly white neighborhood in the suburbs of Lansing, Michigan. No one had ever questioned her heritage and she let them think whatever they wanted.

Her life had been going well and she found no need to disrupt her family. Her two children, Elizabeth and Robert Jr. (whose father was also White) were now adults and barely remembered their other grandmother. They had not made a visit to Albany since Sarah relocated there. Rebecca wanted to put the past in the past. She slowly walked to the mirror that adorned the wall of her chambers and looked at her reflection. Her blonde hair was now streaked with some gray and her tanned skin sparkled with a light film of perspiration as she listened to her mother's voice. The gray-green eyes began to fill with tears because of the lie she was about to tell.

"Mother, that's very nice but I'm afraid I can't make it to your wedding. My calendar for this whole year is full and…" The words caught in her throat.

"But, Dear," Sarah whimpered, "I need you here to help me plan my big day. I need your eyes for a while. Can't you do something?"

The door to her chambers opened and the court clerk said, "Your Honor, they have called your next case."

"Thank you Charles. I'll be right there." Glancing at the telephone receiver she held in her hand, Rebecca said, "I have to go now Mother. I will get back to you. Sorry!" Without waiting for Sarah to respond, Rebecca cradled the receiver and rushed from the room.

Judge St. John looked over the courtroom and felt she should take a lunch break. Her mind was far from where it should be. The decisions she would make in this fraud case would set some precedent and she needed to focus. She banged the gavel and said, "It's almost 11:00 a.m. and now would be a good time to break for lunch."

"But, your Honor," both sides yelled at the same time. "We are ready to proceed with our opening statements. Can't we at least do that before we break?"

"Court is adjourned for one hour," Rebecca said as she banged the gavel without responding to either of the attorneys. The defense threw up his arms in dismay and looked at his client. He was helpless to explain what had just happened. "Women!!!"

"What was that, Mr. Nelson?" Rebecca glanced his way glaring at him.

"Nothing, your Honor, I was just speaking to my client. Sorry."

Rebecca rushed back to her chambers and locked the door behind her. She knew the attorneys were unhappy with her but that was beyond her control and the furthest thing from her mind. How was she going to help her mother and keep her secret? She lay back on her sofa and massaged her temples trying to relieve the growing headache.

The secret had nearly cost her everything she had worked for. She thought back to when it all began, on her 26th birthday, when her boss told her that she was actually her mother, her birth mother. The real estate company she worked for was one of the biggest in Savanna, Georgia and she loved the job hoping to learn all she could about the business. Rebecca had stayed her distance from the woman (her boss) until Sarah Hansen tried to commit suicide. Guilt for her rejection forced her to go to Sarah's side and become part of her life, somewhat.

Her first husband, Robert Lambert, the auto executive, was tolerant of the situation but Rebecca always felt that her heritage had given him license to cheat on her and occasionally abuse her. She stayed with him for ten years because he was her children's father. What a critical error that was. The divorce and custody fight was brutal but nothing about her past came up, surprisingly. She was who she said she was, a white suburban housewife married to a successful man.

The only good thing to come from that ordeal was that the judge on her divorce case was the Honorable Steven St. John, who was now her present husband. During the hearings he counseled her which, while not totally illegal, was definitely unethical because the judge was supposed to be impartial. He made decisions that benefited her financially and made sure that she and Robert had full joint custody of the almost teenagers so that she could be free to pursue their relationship. He had no children and planned to keep it that way.

For days he sat on the bench watching this beautiful blonde woman and fantasized about what could be between them. The widowed judge courted her and convinced her that real estate was not where her future was and that she should go to law school. He knew, however, as a woman in her late twenties, this task would be a huge mountain to climb. Somehow he knew she had the ability if she set her mind to it. With his help and support; she did just that. Between school and raising her two children it was quite a struggle for Rebecca. She was so caught up in Steven's world that her own past became unimportant.

After they were married, there was an occasion when she was in his presence and race was the subject concerning legal matters. She flinched at some of his remarks and opinions and she formed the view on her own that he wouldn't be pleased with her heritage if this information was known; so she didn't bring it up. He had only met her white adoptive parents and they all got along famously. Her two brothers had given him their approval.

She rose from the sofa and once again looked at her reflection in the mirror. Her short bleached-blond hair framed her face like little feathers gathered around her gray-green eyes. Her mocha colored skin glowed. She turned side-ways to look at her pencil thin figure. "Not bad for a 37-year old," she smiled. She didn't want her life to change in any way but she knew it would if she honored her mother's request. Something in her mind said, "Honor thy father and mother that thy days may be long upon the earth. This is the first commandment with a promise." Rebecca caught the end of her desk before she fell having her head reeling. "Which mother?" She questioned.

The timer that she always set for lunch breaks chimed and she knew she had to pull herself together and get back to the trial. "Mr.

Prosecutor, we are ready for your opening statement, then you may call your first witness." Rebecca began as she called the afternoon session to order. She wondered if the courtroom filled with people could see her turmoil. "Do they know?"

The trial proceeded with Rebecca hearing very little of what was being said. "I object, your honor." The defense attorney said. "Overruled," Rebecca said, not really hearing the reason for the objection. She stared at the attorney. "Would you read that back?" She asked the court reporter.

"Overrule this…" someone shouted. Rebecca was startled when she heard the commotion. Had her mind been on the trial, she would have seen the man when he pulled the small caliber weapon from somewhere on his person and point it her way. Next, she felt herself being dragged from the bench;; at the same instance she felt a rush of air pass by her right ear. She was so confused by what was happening her mind didn't comprehend that the defendant in the case had just tried to kill her with a 22 caliber hand gun that had somehow been smuggled into her courtroom. As she lay on the floor behind the podium, her body began to shake uncontrollably and she began to weep. Time seemed to stand still as she listened to all the chaos going on around her.

She tried to right herself but she felt the arms of her bailiff restrain her as he said, "Stay down Judge. We've got him. You're safe; we just need to get this creep out of here. Judge Steve is on his way to you. Just stay calm."

A wave of darkness enveloped her and she lost consciousness. She felt no pain so she knew that she had not been shot but the bullet had missed her head by mere inches. She let her mind go to a safe place until she heard her husband's voice speaking to her.

"Rebecca," Steven St. John whispered. "Darling are you okay? Open your eyes. I'm here. You're safe now.

"Why, what happened…." She stammered. Steven began to explain to her what had occurred. "That maniac on trial evidently didn't like the way things were going so he tried to shoot the Judge. We will get to the bottom of this I assure you."

"How did he get a gun into the courtroom?" Rebecca asked her husband.

"Don't know right now but we'll find out. Don't worry! Let's just go home for the day and thank God that you were not hurt."

Rebecca clung to Steven as he lifted her from the floor and carried her to her chambers behind the courtroom. She trembled as she removed the black robe and put on the light jacket she'd worn that day. She left her ever-present briefcase and all the papers on her desk just as they were and clung to her husband's arm rushing from the room.

The decision she needed to make was evident now. One frightening moment made it all clear that she had to make things right between her and Steven. All the lies and deceit had to desist but that didn't waylay her fears. She was not really ashamed of who she was, she just wanted to avoid conflict or confrontation. She was not good at that. Even some of her cases had caused great emotional upheaval because there had been confrontation on the part of attorneys and herself. She never backed away from a fight but it took her days to get over them. Did that come from Donna's influence; her adopted mother, or did it come from Sarah through heredity? Those are some of the questions she asked herself more than once and until she faced the truth she would never know.

"Steven, we need to talk," Rebecca whispered.

"Not now, Dear," Steven said, pulling her closer to him. "Whatever it is, it can wait."

CHAPTER SEVEN

Sarah held the phone receiver in her hand and thought about her daughter's response when she had asked her for help. Something was very wrong but she would have to trust God for the answer. Her relationship with Rebecca had not been all that Sarah had dreamed but it had been very pleasant and loving, she thought. However, there was so much to do for the wedding, she pushed her feelings aside.

Calvin Logan's apartment was just right for him and Trahn and he felt himself getting somewhat acrimonious when he thought of all the changes that had to be made once he married Sarah. Having made the decision it plagued him as to how he was going to manage taking care of her.

"Have I let my testosterone level make this decision without thinking of the consequences?" While she showed great independence there was so much she couldn't accomplish on her own. She couldn't drive. She couldn't shop on her own. She could put casserole dishes in the oven but she couldn't really cook. Why was he thinking of all the things she couldn't do? She could make him feel the love he needed from her. Sarah could pout her narrow lips and make him want to chew them off her face. She had a way of swinging her hips as she guided her cane that made him quiver, but was that enough? She could manage her own finances, which amazed him. She was very good at handling her duties at school, and she had an amazing singing voice. And she played the piano better than most sighted musicians. What more could he possible want from her? He was still resentful that she had spent most of her adult years with another man and this fact never left him no matter how hard he prayed. Now she had come back to him helpless. He shook his head to clear the hurtful thoughts.

He walked around the rooms to see if there was anything he could do immediately. As he walked through Trahn's bedroom something caught his eye. Amidst all of the clothes and stuff that filled the room, Calvin noticed a large black binder sticking out from under the bed. For some reason, it looked out of place. As he reached down to retrieve it, Trahn opened the door to his room.

"Pops" he began, "what are you doing in my room?" There was a menacing look on his face that Calvin had not observed before.

"I was…" Calvin stammered, "Well, I was just trying to figure out what changes I'm going to have to make to accommodate Sarah."

"You're bringing her here?" Trahn asked.

"Why yes," Calvin answered, "for now because I want her to be able to help me pick a home when it's time. *That* is going to take some doing and time."

"Why don't you do it now?" Trahn asked. "If it's a question of money, I can help you with that."

"Where would you get that kind of money?" Calvin asked smiling at Trahn. "Does that job you have pay you that well?"

"You never know, Pops, you just never know."

Calvin watched as Trahn took his foot and pushed the black folder further under his bed. As Calvin left the room Trahn chided himself for being so careless. "Wow, that was close," he muttered as he took the binder and placed it under some clothes in his closet.

The binder contained a list of all the phony names of the families (that didn't exist) that were receiving large sums of money from the Vietnamese Resource Center. It contained the sums of money allocated to each family and the bank account information where the money had been deposited under Trah and Kim's name but, so far, he had received very little of the proceeds.

Kim had given him just enough funds to keep him in clothes and personal items. He had a nice car and everything he needed and he was hopelessly in love. What more could a man ask for? She had promised that once they had enough they would evenly split what was there. In two years they had accumulated almost one hundred thousand dollars and he was wondering when they would have enough. That was more money than Trahn had ever dreamed of. When he questioned Kim she would only tell him, "Soon, we will have enough very soon." He believed her.

Calvin was troubled. The thought of that folder kept distracting his thoughts. He sat at Sarah's desk at the school and she could sense that something was bothering him. Earlier they had been talking about the things they needed to do before the wedding. They had made some progress but not enough. Sarah had secretly decided that she didn't want an elaborate ceremony but had not asked Calvin how he felt about it.

"Why don't we just elope?" Sarah said jokingly.

Startled, because that is just what he had been thinking, Calvin said, "Are you sure that's what you want?"

"No," she whispered, "I'm not sure, but that's the only thing that makes any sense. We are too old for all of this silliness. Rebecca doesn't seem to have time to come and help me and the students can't see all of the pomp and circumstance so, really, what difference does it make?"

"Besides," Calvin replied, "I'm tired of waiting. Every time I see you I want to ravish you right on the spot. Forgive me Lord," he chuckled.

"Pastor Logan," Sarah said flirtatiously, "My, my, my, what a wonderful thought. Your place, or mine?" They both roared with laughter. He had to see what was in that binder.

He rushed home and Trahn was out. Calvin sat looking at the figures logged in the binder and couldn't figure out what they meant. To him it seemed that Trahn and the center were doing a lot of good for a lot of people. There was no reason for Calvin to know that these people didn't exist.

"Why is Trahn hiding this book?" He asked himself. Circumstances and innuendo surrounding Trahn was beginning to worry him but he was so involved with Sarah and the school that he put all his concerns aside, momentarily.

The trip home to Newport, Tennessee proceeded so smoothly; like it had all been planned and arranged but no preparations had been made on their part. They had applied and received their marriage license and talked to Bishop Logan about the ceremony and hit the road. It was a foregone conclusion that Calvin's father would officiate because this had been talked about more than 30 years before. There were a few flowers, a small cake, some soft inspirational music and two witnesses. Nothing more was needed. Bishop's words were a blur to them both. All they wanted to here was, "I now pronounce you husband and wife." The deep passionate kiss told all present that this marriage was sealed.

When he carried her over the threshold of her mother's home, into the bedroom that had been Sarah's as a young woman, she was transported to another time. It was in the middle of the day and their passion was so strong that the initial lovemaking lasted only moments; both exploding with pent-up emotions and desires. Their bodies shook with passion. After, they lay together face to face clinging to each other exploring every inch of each other's body as if this was their last day on earth and then they came together once again.

The ringing telephone disrupted the tranquility that Sarah felt and languished in. Mabel had given them the house for the weekend so Sarah reluctantly slipped from the bed naked to find the telephone.

"Miss Sarah," Mabel said hesitantly, "Turn on the television and listen to the news."

"Mabel this is my wedding day." Sarah began, "Why would I possibly want to listen to the television?" She chuckled.

"Just turn it on," Mabel insisted.

"This is channel QBYT reporting from Lansing, Michigan where it has just been reported that a local man on trial for fraud has been arrested for the attempted murder of prominent Judge Rebecca St. John as she sat on the bench two days ago. Although the Judge was not injured, she has not been back into her courtroom since the incident. Stay tuned for more details as they become available."

"Calvin," Sarah screamed. "Come quickly. Something has happened to Rebecca."

Sarah had spoken of her so seldom that it took Calvin a moment to realize that Sarah was talking about her daughter, her only child. He immediately took her in his arms to quiet her shaking. "I have to go to her," Sarah muttered. "Please get me to her."

It was her wedding night and Sarah didn't sleep at all. She felt so helpless, so inadequate, knowing that even when she got to her daughter, there was nothing she could do for her. She had long ago lost touch with her grown-up grandchildren, Elizabeth and Robert so she didn't know how to contact either of them. When she expressed all of these doubts and fears to Calvin he simply said, "Have faith, Sarah." This infuriated her because this statement seemed to say that she had no faith which was not the case, or was it? She moved further to her side of the car and they continued their journey in silence as she reflected upon; what? Everything and nothing! This is not how she had envisioned spending her first full day of marriage to Calvin Logan. She had not even had time to get used to her new name, Sarah Elaine Logan.

CHAPTER EIGHT

When they arrived in Lansing, after a longer than normal drive, Sarah suddenly realized that she didn't know where Rebecca lived. She only had a phone number or two, one for her cell phone and one for her office. Calvin was incredulous and wanted to ask her how she could have neglected to get an address but he knew this was not a good time.

"You don't have an address?" He asked patiently. "So you can call her?"

"Yes, Calvin, I can call her," she said reaching for her specially made cell phone with the raised numbers on the face.

Calvin pulled up into a near-by gas station to fill the tank up and waited silently while Sarah attempted to reach Rebecca. As he returned to the car he noticed the expression on Sarah's face.

He heard her say, "Yes, Rebecca I'm here in Lansing. I heard on the news about what happened. Why didn't you call me or have someone else call me? Tell me where you are? I don't have your address, you know. What?" Sarah said. "We are in a service station somewhere. Wouldn't it be better just to give me the address to your home and we can come there?"

Calvin watched as the tears began to flow from under her dark glasses. "Okay, Rebecca, we'll wait for you here." He took the phone and gave the woman on the other end the address of the service station. He didn't want to speculate about what that conversation meant. He waited for an explanation from Sarah.

"She wants to meet me here." Sarah said nothing more. He waited.

"I don't understand," Sarah began. "It would be so easy for us to go to her so she could rest but..." her voice trailed off.

The location must have been close because in less than 30 minutes Calvin saw this very nice metallic red Mercedes automobile pull into the station. He knew right away that it was Rebecca because the license

42

plate bore the name 'JUDGE S-2'. He watched as she exited the car and walked towards where they were parked.

He observed a younger version of Sarah with much lighter skin and smaller body. Had he not known who she was, he would have mistaken her for a white woman. He noticed that her face was pale and that she had been crying. She ignored him and went to the passenger side of the car, opened the door and fell into her mother's arms, kissing her face. They both began to weep loudly. Calvin was stunned and walked away so they could be alone. He wanted no part of this drama.

"He doesn't know about you," Rebecca began.

"Who are you talking about?" Sarah asked.

"Steven, my husband, doesn't know about you yet. I had planned to tell him but all of this happened and I never got the chance. I know it was a mistake to disavow who I am but that was not my intentions, it just never came up." She looked at her mother sheepishly. "I wanted to come here first and explain before you meet him. I'm so sorry now and I wanted to give you a choice as to what we will tell him when I take you home."

"We'll tell him the truth," Sarah said . While Calvin loitered inside the station the two women talked about the turns Rebecca's life had taken since their last reunion. Sarah tried to comprehend but her heart was broken.

"I'm trying to grasp what you're telling me but it's very hard," Sarah whimpered. "Let's go meet this Steve, she said, grasping Rebecca's hand in hers.

When Calvin saw Rebecca exit the car he walked towards where she stood. He reached his hand towards her expecting a hand-shake and said, "I'm Calvin Logan."

Instead she threw her arms around his neck, gave him a tight hug and said, "Yes, I know exactly who you are. Thank you for bringing her to me!"

"No need. My pleasure." Calvin said as he returned her hug.

"Follow me," she said.

After a short drive Calvin whispered to Sarah, "We're here."

"Tell me what the house looks like," Sarah said.

Calvin observed a very modest home, nothing like what he expected. It was a Tudor style bungalow with a huge bay window in the front loaded with flowers that could be seen from the outside. Attached was a two car garage with one side door opened. The lawn was professionally manicured and the flowers immaculate. In the driveway was the twin to the Mercedes that Rebecca drove with the license plate name "JUDGE S-1. As Rebecca pulled into the garage and shut the door remotely, he helped Sarah from the car and they both stood at the front door. Shortly Rebecca opened the front door and behind her stood Steven with a not so pleasant look on his face. He stood about 6'3"tall with a full head of graying red hair. His eyes were bright blue and his jaw was set stern. Sarah sensed the tension and as Rebecca began to make the introductions, she unfolded her white cane, took a few steps into the doorway, extended her hand and said.

"My name is Sarah Logan and I am Rebecca's former employer. She worked for me and my late husband when we were in real estate in Savannah, GA. I heard about her misfortune on the news and my husband and I were in the area so I thought I'd come by and pay my respects. I hope this is not a bad time."

Calvin and Rebecca stood stunned listening as Sarah told the story. They both couldn't protest because everything that she said was the truth, if only a half-truth. They couldn't make sense of this. Rebecca had been resigned to tell Steven the truth and let the chips fall where they may, now it had once again been delayed. She didn't know how to feel about this. She had wanted to have back-up when she confronted him but now...

Steven's whole countenance changed when he heard Sarah's explanation as to why they were at his home. Before he closed the front door, however, he glanced up and down the street to see if any of the neighbors happened to see Calvin come into his residence. He was like a fly in the buttermilk.

When they had settled in the huge library filled with thousands of Law books and others; while Calvin described it to her, Sarah thought of the library she had seen all those years ago and flinched at the thought. She was recalling the night Rebecca had been conceived. Calvin felt her reaction and asked, "Are you okay?"

"I'm fine," she whispered. "You have a lovely home, Rebecca, may I have a tour?"

"Of course," Rebecca blushed. She instantly reached for her mother's arm to guide her. When they arrived to the bedroom, Rebecca quickly closed the door and said, "Mother, what are you doing? Why didn't you let me tell him while I have the courage? Now I can't tell him and make a liar of you."

"I don't know," Sarah said, "the time just doesn't seem right and this is a decision you have to make on your own and I'm sure you will make the right choice."

"But Mother, I need your help with this. Tell me what to do?"

"I can't," Sarah said, remembering the times she had said those exact words to her own mother and not getting an answer. She turned abruptly away from her daughter and immediately bumped into something in her path. She heard Rebecca gasp and immediately told her, "I'm fine. I do this all the time." Both women laughed and went to the next room. As they passed the huge mirror that hung in the hallway, Rebecca noticed how remarkable the resemblance was. How could she ever deny that fact? Steven most assuredly has noticed.

The rest of the visit went quickly to Sarah. She noticed that Steven kept raising his voice every time he spoke to her. Finally she said to him, "Steven, there is no need to raise your voice. I am only blind, I'm not deaf too." There came a nervous laughter from all. This seemed to set the tone for the rest of the visit and everyone seemed more relaxed but Sarah was fuming on the inside. It still amazed her at the ignorance of some people who thought that if a person is blind he or she also has to be deaf.

"Help me Lord," she whispered.

They discussed what had happened in the courtroom and the upcoming trial Rebecca would have to attend to prosecute this man. For her safety, Rebecca's calendar had been cleared for the next six months and she and Steve were talking about her relocating, possibly to another state.

Calvin watched the two women interact with each other and couldn't understand why Steve didn't see what he saw. It was very obvious that their relationship was far more than just employee and employer. And the resemblance was remarkable and unmistakable.

Calvin saw that it was getting late and he asked Rebecca about a hotel where they could stay for the night. She hesitated for a moment hoping that Steven would extend an invitation for them to stay with them. When that didn't happen, Rebecca handed Calvin a card with a local hotel address on it. "This is a very nice place," she said handing the card to Calvin. "Please call me before you leave the city," she said facing her mother.

"Of course we will," Sarah said, reaching for her daughter. Rebecca glanced at Calvin and then at Steven and decided to brush her mother's cheek instead of hugging her neck. Sarah understood!

CHAPTER NINE

While Sarah and Calvin were away from Albany, Trahn decided that now would be a good time for him to move from Calvin's apartment before things got out of hand. He knew he couldn't hide his records from Calvin forever. Things were going too well for him to mess up now. He felt that any day now Kim was going to get a divorce from Pho and marry him. He needed to have a place to take her once she made that decision and then all of this would be over. They would be together and their schemes would be ending.

He found a place close to the Resource Center and told Kim. She was elated that she would have him under her full control and thought that he would have no more dealings with Calvin or that school but Trahn had other plans.

The school continued to be a source for extra money and companionship. When he couldn't see Kim, which was more often than not, he continued to date Anna and take from her all that she had to give including her virginity. Her blindness was an asset to him and he took full advantage of it.

The students were starting to whisper among themselves because they knew far more than everyone gave them credit for and, of course, like most women her age, Anna had no secrets. She gushed every time she heard Trahn's name mentioned or heard his voice.

Director Sam Smith had also gotten wind of the affair and was troubled. He had decided to talk to Calvin about the matter once he returned. With Calvin gone he saw no reason for Trahn to be there. He noticed one day that Anna was wearing a new ring that he didn't recognize. It was his job to keep good contact and rapport with the students while they were on campus and to take notice of anything unusual.

He stopped her in the hall one day and said, "Anna is that a new ring you're wearing?"

"Yes it is," Anna gushed. "Trahn gave it to me." She said without hesitation.

"Why would he give you such an expensive ring?" Sam asked watching for her reaction.

"Because we are friends and he likes me." Anna said blushing.

"Is your mother okay with that?" Sam asked

"Of course, she loves Trahn." Anna said as she continued to her classroom. To Sam, the matter was closed because Anna was a full grown woman despite living with her mother, but it troubled him none-the-less.

The moment they walked into his apartment Calvin knew that something was amiss. He told Sarah, "I'm not going to carry you over this threshold because this will not be our home for long. We will buy a home when you find one you like."

"How am I going to do that?" Sarah asked punching him on the arm. "Oh," Calvin laughed. "We'll think of something."

He deposited the suitcases they had with them and went to Trahn's room calling his name as he went. When he opened the door to the room he noticed that everything was gone. Not only Trahn's clothing, but the furniture Calvin had purchased for the room was also gone.

"Is Trahn in his room?" Sarah asked.

"No, he's not in his room; looks like he's moved out."

"Moved out?" Sarah repeated. "Is it because of me? Did you know he was leaving?"

"No to both questions." Calvin whispered. "We didn't discuss this at all. She could hear the sadness and disappointment in his voice. She was hoping her joy didn't show on her face. She didn't relish sharing a space with Trahn. The distrust she had for him had not lessened in the least.

"Maybe he'll call tomorrow," Sarah said. "Now show me to our bedroom," Sarah snickered with a mischievous smile on her face.

When they returned to work, Calvin could see and Sarah could feel the tension in the air. There were whispers that Anna had not been in school for a few days and her mother didn't seem to know where she was. Anna had called her mother and told her that she wanted to get away for a few days and that she was doing well where ever she was. Anna's mother told the school that she had done this before and that she had been able to take care of herself just fine and for them not to worry; she would return soon.

Everyone knew but none spoke of the fact that she might be with Trahn. They had no authority or reason to call the authorities since Anna's mother seemed not to be worried about her daughter's safety but everyone at the school was tense.

"He gave her a diamond ring," Sam began as he talked to Calvin and Sarah.

"He did what?" Calvin yelled.

"I saw it on her finger myself. She was very happy to tell me that Trahn had given it to her because they were friends. Do you think he would do something so stupid as to steal her away from her mother?"

"I don't think he would have to steal her," Sarah said. "Anna is quite taken with him. It wouldn't take much persuasion on his part. If she's not back in school by Friday, we will look for her. The choir has a performance on Saturday and she has a lead song."

"When he calls you" she said turning towards Calvin, "find out where he is."

"If he calls," Calvin whispered.

A week after Sarah moved into Calvin's apartment things were finally beginning to feel comfortable and familiar. Calvin had placed things in her path that she could use as guides to each room as well as the kitchen. All of the appliances had been fitted with Braille dots so that she could operate them safely and she felt like a regular housewife and felt very independent.

Calvin, however, had not anticipated how much help Sarah really needed and sometimes became exasperated at having to stop his plans to drive her where she needed to go and to help with shopping and cleaning. He was becoming overwhelmed and he wondered if his love for her was enough to sustain him. It was getting more difficult to suppress his disappointment that they were not going to have a normal life together ever. He often found himself saying to her, "What do you want from me?"

While standing at the refrigerator with the door ajar, Sarah thought she heard a noise. She stood still trying to hear it again, and when she didn't, she continued with what she was doing. Trahn stood at the front door watching her as she maneuvered about the kitchen. He had not closed it right away because he knew that she would detect him. She jumped when she heard the door shut. "Who's there?" she said. She knew that Calvin was at the school and she became frightened. "Calvin is that you?" She tried again. Trahn stifled a giggle as he watched her frightened expression.

"I could do anything I wanted to her right now. She is so pretty; and that body. Pops is a lucky man. I might take her money but I won't stoop that low as to touch her," Trahn sighed.

She screamed when she felt the hand touch her arm. "Calm down, Sarah, it's me Trahn. I let myself in with my key. I used to live here remember?"

"Trahn," she screamed, why didn't you answer me? Were you trying to frighten me?"

"No way," he said. I was just watching you make your way around this kitchen. You are amazing."

He felt her jump when he took her hand. "I just came by to see Pops. Is he here?"

"You know that he's at the school this time of day, or have you forgotten?"

Before she knew it she yelled, "Where is Anna?"

"Whoo," he said. "How would I know where Anna is? She's at the school isn't she?

"She's not and I think you know that."

"Nope, don't know a thing about that," he said. "Tell Pops I stopped by and I'll call him soon. Take care of yourself, Sarah." She then heard the front door close and she stopped shaking. She immediately picked up the cell phone that lay on the kitchen table and dialed Calvin's number.

He could hear the panic in her voice and asked, "Sarah is everything okay?"

"Yes, I'm fine. I just wanted to tell you that Trahn was just here and he scared to devil out of me. He left without leaving his key."

"Did he say where he's been or if he's seen Anna?"

"He says he hasn't seen her but I don't believe him. He didn't tell me where he's living. He just told me to tell you that he would call you soon. Can you come home now?"

"Not yet Sarah," He said, "I'm in the middle of a session. I'll be there soon." He sat and rubbed his temple.

Trahn returned to his little apartment, opened the door and got the shock of his life. Standing in the middle of the floor was Kim and Anna in deep conversation. When she heard the door open, Anna immediately said, "Trahn honey, your boss is here to see you.

"Yes, Trahn, your boss is here to see you," Kim said with a look that could kill.

When Anna left the room Kim spat, "Who is the Chippy?"

"Oh she's just one of the girls from school, Baby. She just needed a place to crash for a few days." He reached to take her into his arms. As they kissed, Anna returned to the room totally unaware of what was going on two feet in front of her. She didn't see the look of hatred Kim gave her as she closed the front door as she left.

"She's a nice lady," Anna said as she sat back down in the chair she always occupied.

"When are you going home?" Trahn asked angrily.

"I thought you wanted me here," Anna said innocently.

"I did but now it's time for you to return home. They are asking questions at the school. I don't want any trouble there."

"Well, if you marry me like you said, I could stay with you forever," Anna said beginning to cry.

"Stop it Anna, you're not ready for that yet." He bawled his fist wanting to strike her.

"You have used me for these weeks and now you want to send me home? What kind of game are you playing with me, Trahn? You said you loved me!" She was now weeping openly.

"You see, that's what I'm talking about. We have a few weeks of fun and you want to turn it into a lifetime commitment. Lighten up and enjoy. You can stay as long as you like, but don't ask me to commit to anything." He pulled her to him and she melted in his arms.

Kim was not happy. Even though she knew about his work at the school, she thought since he had moved into his own place that he was through with all that. She didn't believe for one second that Anna was just a friend needing a place to crash. "Blind people don't just crash," she thought. While Pho was her husband, Trahn was her "boy toy" and she didn't want to share him with anyone. Besides, he was her money maker. Just as she thought, with his upbringing, he was just right for the scheme she hatched. She knew he couldn't resist the lure of fast money and she was sure that he wouldn't require much. On the other hand she had fallen hard for his lovemaking. There was no comparison between Trahn and Pho. No comparison! The more she thought of Anna and Trahn together the madder she became. She would have to fix this problem.

PART II

CHAPTER TEN
"THE CHURCH"

When Bishop Logan made the trip from Newport to Albany his purpose was two-fold. He really wanted to see how Calvin and Sarah were getting on but he also wanted to share some news with the two of them. He had decided that after 50 years it was time for him to step down from the pulpit of his church and he desperately wanted Calvin to take his place. Now that he and Sarah were married he felt that it was a necessity for Calvin to fulfill the calling God had on his life. He was not sure if Calvin knew it or acknowledged it or even wanted it but he had to remind him of the promise he made to Calvin's mother on the day of his birth. She willingly surrendered her life so that Calvin could live and follow in his father's footsteps.

He could understand why they liked it there in Albany. What he observed on his few visits to Calvin was that the city was quite nice and their work was very rewarding. The students seemed to care a lot for him and especially Sarah. They hadn't purchased a home yet so he figured they hadn't set any deep roots. He saw that they were deeply in love but that Calvin was a little stressed. He wanted to see if his faith was waning. Bishop hadn't seen a great falling away from what he was taught, as a child and in Seminary, but Calvin seemed a little unsure of his standing with God.

He watched as Calvin taught a weekly Bible lesson to the students and knew that he was doctrinally sound. He observed how he easily interacted with others when there was a crisis, except when it came to Trahn. He seemed to flounder when it came to Trahn.

He had been in Albany a week when he shared his plans. Sarah and Calvin seemed stunned when they heard the news. It was the last thing they expected to hear. Calvin thought that his father would have to be pulled from the pulpit kicking and screaming or either flat of his back, never by his own will.

"Son, I think it's time for you to take your rightful place at the Temple of The Living God Community Church. I don't know if you have accepted your call from God or if you're running from it, but now it's time. The church is strong and I don't want to leave the congregation without a pastor. I won't leave until you have made a decision. Pray about it, Son."

"Wow," Calvin replied. "What brought this on? Are you ill? I never thought I'd see the day."

"I'm 85-years-old, Calvin. We all get to retire sometime. I'm tired. I miss your mother and I want to rest. Is that so hard to understand?"

Calvin knew that he meant every word he spoke. Now he had another decision to make. He took Sarah's hand as he said, "Dad, we'll pray about it."

"I await your call," Bishop said as he hugged Sarah and his son good-by and made his way onto the plane for the trip back to Newport. He was at peace.

The decision to move was not as hard to make as Calvin and Sarah thought. "What will we tell Sam?" Calvin dreaded what they were about to do. He knew somehow that the last few years of his life had been leading to this. Marrying Sarah had been the last piece to the puzzle and now all things were set in place except for Trahn. What would he do about Trahn? He still felt a great obligation to him. His year was up for his Visa stay so Calvin was no longer legally responsible for him but there was something stronger. He wanted to see him settled before he left Albany but that didn't seem to be happening. There was little discussion between Sarah and Calvin. They both knew what the choice would be so Sarah set her mind for a new adventure. She was not afraid of the change. Somehow she knew the adjustment would be seamless. Her life had come full circle and she was looking forward to a new challenge but she would certainly miss her students.

They promised Sam that they would give him one month to find their replacements. They told Mabel that they would need to move into Sarah's home for a short time until they found their own. Sarah had long-ago decided to give Mabel her mother's home that was fully paid for and she would do that as soon as possible. So far they had told Trahn nothing. Calvin didn't know what to say to him. He would give him the option of coming with them but somehow he knew Trahn would reject the invitation and so would Sarah. He was beginning to see the deep mistrust she had for him and this distressed him greatly.

Excitement filled her heart when Sarah began to pack up Calvin's apartment. She asked him to describe every piece they packed into boxes. Calvin's heart was heavy and he was weary of talking.

"Sarah, can we do this when we get there?" he asked exasperated. "I will tell you all that we have then. Right now, let's just get it all done."

"Sorry, Dear, I just wanted to know what we have. I won't ask again."

"*WE* don't have anything," he thought. He thought of Diana and quickly pushed her image from his thoughts. They had purchased all that he had together and he didn't want to share that with Sarah but she had so many questions. So many questions!!!

Calvin noticed the sad look on her face and gently touched her cheek. "I know, Sarah, I know." He'd noticed lately how easy it was to snap at her and hurt her feelings. He just wished she could fight back.

The day they were to leave, Anna returned to school still not admitting that she and Trahn were living together. Sarah hugged her tightly never imagining that this would be the last time she would have contact with her. She begged her to take care of herself and keep in touch and she could feel the sadness coming from Anna.

"You'll be alright," Sarah whispered in Anna's ear as she hugged her one last time. Anna didn't have the heart to tell Calvin and Sarah how unhappy she was with Trahn and ruin their trip.

From the shadows Trahn watched all of this transpire. He purposely had not answered any of the calls placed to him by Calvin. There would be no good-by on his part. He felt that he was no longer part of Calvin's life and that was fine with him. His face was moist with tears as he clenched his jaw as well as his fists. "Good riddance," he said to no one in particular.

Sarah seemed to be especially clingy as they drove the U-Haul truck away from Sarah's Place towing Calvin's car behind it. She sat as close to him as she could with the divider separating them, and she touched his leg over and over again. She tried very hard to be light-hearted and happy but he heard her sniffles. He wondered if he was making a mistake but he kept driving. "God will make a way," he repeated. But his heart asked the question, "What have I done?"

Sarah felt more tranquil as she walked through the rooms of her old home. Everything was familiar and she knew every space in the house. It was strange how she could see with her minds-eye all the furnishings that filled each room. It was small but it suited her perfectly. She guessed that Calvin wouldn't be comfortable here and would find them a house soon. She would enjoy this while she could.

Mabel had left everything clean and ready for them to move right in. All they needed were their personal belongings and the rest of Calvin's furniture was put into a temporary storage facility. The home that the church supplied for Calvin's father was much too small to hold his things and he wanted his father to stay there for the duration.

It had been a long tedious drive and they were both exhausted. She thought it was the excitement when she felt her heart skip a beat and dizziness overtook her. She slept fitfully that night and clung to Calvin as never before. She noticed that he kept pushing her hand away as he slept. She wanted him to hold her and make the pain go away. She turned her face toward the wall and prayed and soon she was fast asleep holding to the edge of the bed.

Sarah Logan's life was drastically changing and she knew that this is where God wanted her to be but she couldn't shake the apprehension she felt about becoming a Pastor's wife. When she and Calvin had been re-united she realized there was that possibility. Never-the-less the thought of helping Calvin pastor a church while blind seemed like an impossible daunting task that she was not ready for. The dream was frightening and she woke drenched in sweat. "What is it?" She couldn't remember.

CHAPTER ELEVEN
"THE MIRACLE"

Board members and staff of the church sat sternly in their appointed places around the huge conference table and listened to the Bishop lay out the schedule for this Sunday's services. The seating arrangements and pecking order never varied. Those who felt they were closest to the bishop sat close to him at the table, and so forth. Their faces showed the distaste they felt about the decision Bishop Logan had made about his retirement. They all had an agenda.

Lois Lovealot, the church secretary, sat at the bishop's right hand and it would take a bomb blast to move her. The 70-something year old spinster was secretly in love with the bishop and wanted desperately to be with him no matter where he went. She couldn't imagine his stepping down from the pulpit as this would diminish her power.

Whoever the new pastor was going to be, he undoubtedly would bring in his own staff and she would be out. "That can't happen," she thought. She had devoted most of her adult life to the ministry and to Bishop without (what she thought) the proper recognition. "No, he won't get away with that." She shook with anger. Lois knew where all the skeletons were buried and she had her shovel ready to dig them all up if necessary. "Don't mess with me!" She almost spoke aloud. She glanced around the table to make sure none of the others had heard her thoughts.

Vera Mae Sassy, the head of the Praise Team, as everybody referred to her, and the devoted 45-year-old wife of Deacon Sassy, mother of eight, was not worried in the least. Her position was secure because nobody could do what she did. She could shout with the best of them and stir the congregation up like none other. She would show that new pastor that she was indispensable, irreplaceable or else.

Deacon Jeremiah Samuelson was unusually quiet. While his demeanor was sullen, his mind was racing like 30 going north. His tummy was jumping and felt like it was giggling on the inside. "It's about time that old goat stepped down." His stomach made a strange sound and everyone looked his way. "Just a little gas," he replied. He was so tired of 'having the bishop's back.' Jeremiah always felt like he did more than the bishop did and that he was really the pastor of the church without the title. Most of the congregation called upon him when there was an issue they had to deal with. "My fifteen-year old is pregnant." Well, call Deacon Jeremiah. "I can't pay my rent this month." Call Deacon. "My husband came home drunk again last night." Call Deacon. "I'm sick, sick, and sick of it. Now everybody will see who really does the work around here." His stomach gurgled again. "The new pastor can have his duties and I can rest," that was his thinking.

Missus Snowden, the choir director, Sunday school teacher, board member and all-around 'Ms. Fixit' was elated at the news but she really didn't know why. Nearing 80 years herself she had no intentions of stepping down from anything. She had been doing these duties in the church for 40 years and none of the changes had affected her one way or the other. They couldn't make her become more contemporary with her song selections or waver in her teachings to accommodate the young people.

"The young people need to adjust to the word of God", was her favorite saying and she repeated it often. She was praying that the new pastor would see things her way or she would have to pull some strings with God. With all the blessings she'd experienced in her life she was assured that she could get a prayer through. "Hallelujah." None of the members were startled by her anymore when she yelled out her praise at some inappropriate time with her hands waving about in the air.

The rest of the board members, deacons and staff sat quietly non-committal and totally disinterested in what was going on around them. Their attention was garnered only when Bishop announced that his son Calvin would be the new pastor.

"Ain't that some sort of nepotism? Shouldn't we have some say about who's gonna' be our next pastor?" Some inquired.

"Ain't never had no say before; why should this be any different?" Someone else responded.

"Is he saved?" others asked.

"Of course he's saved," Bishop responded. He's been to Seminary and is an ordained Elder in the church.

"That don't mean nothing now-a-days," Someone else responded.

"Is he married?" Vera Mae asked.

"He is. As a matter of fact, he's married to that Justin girl from right here in Newport, uh Sarah, you all remember her?" Some didn't and some did remember.

"Ain't her daddy that white man; what was his name again?"

"Yes, her father was Paul Justin and her mother was Suzanne Williams, what about it? Both of them are gone now."

"Don't know if I want no half-breed over me."

"Who said that?" Bishop raised his voice. There was no response.

"If there is anyone else at this table who feels that way, let the door hit you in the back. This is a Christian meeting and we will conduct ourselves as such. We are living in a new millennium and that kind of talk and 'stinkin' thinkin' will not be tolerated. Besides, I built this church from the ground, didn't I Missus Snowden, and you all will do as I say and that's how it's going to be.

"Yes, and that fund-raising lasted a whole generation," someone whispered. Someone else giggled. Since the bishop was now hard of hearing, that comment got past him.

"One last question, Bishop, is that boy going to come in here and change everything we done built over these 50 years?" Missus Snowden sniffed as if to squash a tear.

"That will be completely up to him," Bishop said. "This meeting is adjourned." He rose from his seat to leave the room with Lois Lovealot right on his heels.

"Let's pray! Help us Lord," Deacon Jeremiah bowed his head.

"I don't know about y'all but I ain't worried in the least 'cause he cain't do without me and that's a fact."

"Oh hush up, Vera Mae."

"Don't have to," Vera Mae said throwing her large head into the air and strutting out the door.

That was the make-up of the Temple of the Living God Community Apostolic Church of Newport.

Sarah and Calvin had been waiting in the bishop's office for their cue to join the meeting, however, when Bishop stormed through the door they didn't know what they should do.

"Go on in there if you want," he said to them, but be forewarned, some of them ain't too happy with me right about now."

When Calvin and Sarah walked through the door of the conference room they were greeted with a loud chorus of, "Praise the Lord, Welcome Elder and First Lady, Glory to God."

"Dear Lord, she blind," someone whispered. "Dear Jesus, what we gonna' do now?"

"Oh Dear!! What do we do?" Calvin whispered in Sarah's ear. Sarah giggled, "You're asking me!!!"

Months passed without incident and only a few members left. When Elder Calvin Logan sat down with Sister Lovealot to ascertain their financial status, he was pleasantly surprised to find that the church had $80,000 dollars in the bank with no outstanding debt except the $100,000 dollar mortgage. Their standing in the community was strong and Calvin knew that he could build if he only had some help. He thought of Sarah. "What about Sarah?" The Bishop was given the title of Senior Pastor and he attended church if and when he felt like it but Sis. Lovealot saw him daily having taken on the duty of supplying the Bishop with in-home care which carried with it a generous salary supplied by the church. All was well with Lois.

"I know everything about this church so you just ask me whatever it is you want to know," she told Elder Logan. "Folks say that I know where all the secrets lay but I don't know about that," she said with a mischievous grin on her lips.

"I'll keep that in mind, Sis. Lois" Elder Logan believed she knew it all.

That Sunday when Sarah received her miracle, the sanctuary was filled to capacity. For some unexplained reason, Rebecca was there along with her daughter Elizabeth and son Bobby. She hadn't told Sarah of her plans and had come to town unannounced. No one except Calvin recognized her when she walked into the sanctuary.

There was a stir when the supposed white woman made her entrance. That was a rare occurrence. Vera Mae Sassy had whipped the whole church into a frenzy and the whole atmosphere changed in an instant. The congregation couldn't get past the worship and Deacon Jeremiah was worried that Elder Logan was not going to get to his sermon on time.

To Calvin, there seemed to be a mist in the air that covered his podium. He sat in his chair in total reverence; feeling that something powerful was about to happen. He glanced at Sarah and noticed that she was trying to rise from her seat but was having some sort of difficulty.

Sister Lovealot also noticed that one of the deacons was kneeling on all fours before the altar in prayer and the rest of the congregation was starting to fall upon their faces in worship. "What is going on?" She asked the woman that stood next to her. Calvin also became caught up in whatever was going on in the church and didn't notice that Sarah was walking towards him without her cane. Her dark glasses were gone and he saw her gray eyes staring in his direction as she walked up the steps that led to the pulpit.

His heart nearly exploded with gladness when Sarah told him that she could see his face. "In your sermon last week you told us all to have faith and not give up. Was that message for me?"

"I suppose it was," Calvin could hear his own heart beating loudly.

Sarah took his face into her hands and said, "I thank God for you Elder Logan."

When the congregation finally became aware of what had just occurred, there are no words to describe the mood that surrounded the members except pure unadulterated JOY! Most of them had never experienced such an event in their entire lives and sat there unbelieving yet seeing the miracle with their own eyes. There was no sermon preached that Sunday!

When news of the miracle spread Calvin had to start a new building fund because the church was filled to overflowing every Sunday for an entire year, then the glory wore off and things returned to normal. Once again people were getting offended; friends were talking about each other and complaining that the pastor and first lady were not doing the will of God as they saw it. Now, Sarah could see the distress in her husband's face and also the relief that now he had someone to share it with.

Sarah slipped into her role smoothly and very few changes had to be made except now there was a rumor floating around that said one of the deacons had an unusual interest in the First Lady. There were comments being made like; "That was no miracle, I think she could see all the time, just trying to fool us and, of course, the Elder fell for it. She has always been some kind of anomaly here in Newport. Y'all just don't know. We need to watch her!"

CHAPTER TWELVE
"STEVEN"

Rebecca's near death experience had a profound effect on how she made decisions from the bench and court authorities were beginning to notice. The toughness, assertiveness and decisiveness were gone. Her husband Steven had no answer for the questions that bombarded him. He was as confused as the rest. He had seen a great change in her at home as well. That confident, out-going woman that he fell in love with was missing. He often found her brooding and secretive as if she were guarding something from him.

He understood that the incident in the courtroom had frightened her but this was something more. There were age lines beginning to show in her once smooth face. He struggled to find a way to pull her out of this funk, this malaise.

Judge Steven St. John was now the chief justice of the Michigan Supreme Court; well respected, fair and totally full of himself. His stature was erect and pride oozed from every pore. He was 6'3" tall and weighed a good 300 pounds. His bright red hair, now streaked with gray, was like a beacon in the night. His deep brown eyes exuded stability and reliability. The Harvard Law School graduate, Sum e-Cum-Laud, had risen to the top in short order. Graduation, law practice, judgeship, marriage, Supreme Court; accomplished all in less than 20 years. Not many people from the small town of Mason, Ohio had accomplished such a feat.

He no longer thought about or talked about his immediate family whose history he'd just recently unearthed. After doing a genealogy check for a bio for an upcoming tribute, Steven had found some disturbing things in his background. It sees that his great grandfather, twice removed, was once a leader in the Underground Railroad that passed through Ohio during slavery times. It also appeared that he had taken a liking to one of the black slave women that escaped north to freedom.

Remembering from his childhood the whispered stories that circulated at family gatherings, although there was no marriage, it appeared there was an offspring born from this attachment which led directly to Steven's grandfather. Along with Rebecca, he too was troubled by his family history.

At meetings and gatherings of his colleges, it was a given that Steven St. John would be the life of the party with his racial jokes. While on the outside he appeared just as liberal as the next man when it came to racial issues, on the inside his soul was Lillie white.

When he met Rebecca; the pretty slightly tanned skin and beautiful gray-green eyes were the features that drew him to her. Since he'd dealt in litigation with the auto industry in Detroit, he knew very well who her ex-husband was.

They first appeared before him in the struggle for a divorce and custody of their two children. Though not totally against the law, it was very unethical for him to take an interest and guide her through the process, although he felt he had been quite fair in his decisions as far as division of the property, the children were another matter.

He was unmarried and was seeking a companion unencumbered with baggage and to him, children were baggage. He had decided long ago that his legacy or bloodline would end with him. The information he received about his heritage only convinced him that he was right. His rulings in Rebecca's case made liberal concessions to Robert Lambert as far as the custody of his then almost teenaged children was concerned. He awarded equal custody to both parents assuring that Rebecca would have plenty of time for his advances. Of course the awarding of assets was very generous toward Rebecca so that she would be independent. He loved it when a plan came together!!!

In her early 30's Steven realized that Rebecca was a little long in the tooth to be beginning law school but he could pull some strings. He knew her looks and his power could open lots of doors and she would be in his debt. All of his expectations were met and more.

It took less than five years for her to become a circuit court judge. Right now, however, things were beginning to deteriorate and he was losing control. Out of the blue, at the dinner table of their elaborately furnished home, with Emma the cook and maid standing nearby, Rebecca told him that she needed to take a trip to Newport, Tennessee. She told him some ridiculous story about Bobby, her son, having some sort of outing that she needed to participate in. It was not unusual for Rebecca to go on these "get-a-ways" as she referred to them and be gone for a few days but never for a week. Something was up, he could feel it.

"I can take a few days off, why don't I come with you?" He said watching her eyes closely.

"That won't be necessary dear," she purred. "I just need to get away from here for a little while so I can clear my mind of the last month. You understand, don't you?"

He didn't understand but he said, "Yea, I guess so." He had decided that he would follow her.

"Are you going to drive?" Steven asked.

"Yes, I'm going to pick up Elizabeth in Detroit so she can help me drive down to Tennessee."

That's a great idea."

Rebecca didn't notice the black rental car following her.

She and Elizabeth were deep in conversation and she was relieved to see her mother in such good spirits.

"We're going to visit your grandmother, Sarah," Rebecca told her daughter when she entered the car.

"I figured as much," Elizabeth said. "I don't know anybody else in Newport other than some long lost cousin. That's great. I have not seen her in a very long time and I miss that." Reluctantly she asked, "Is she still blind?"

"Elizabeth!!" Sarah giggled. "What a silly thing to say. Of course she is."

"I'm just asking."

The black car pulled on to the side of the road and waited for the Mercedes to fill up with gas. When the car pulled away from the pump the man pulled in and filled the tank and quickly peeled out behind the Mercedes. The two women noticed nothing unusual. Rebecca had decided to drive straight through except stops for gas and rest areas and the trip went smoothly with them sharing their memories of other visits they had made to Sarah while she was in Savanna, Georgia, long before Steven.

They didn't talk about the father that Elizabeth adored or about Steven who she took with a grain of salt, this was their time together. They discussed where they would stay because they were going to surprise Sarah with their visit. Johnny was to meet them there. They were both excited about visiting Sarah and Calvin's new church. Not having been in his presence much, they both had heard the stories of their long and lasting love for each other and they were both overjoyed at what had unfolded.

"Their story sounds like a fairy tale," Elizabeth told her mother. "Nobody comes back together after all of those years and then this??? That's hard to believe."

"Well it's all true, Rebecca said, "and you will hear the story for yourself."

When they entered the sanctuary of The Church of the Living God, Elizabeth drew closer to her mother. She had never seen such goings on at church. The church she attended in Detroit was very quiet and very conservative. Their congregation would never behave in such a manner. "Have these people gone mad?" She asked her mother.

"No," Rebecca said, this is what's called 'praising God'. This is how they do it in the Apostolic or holiness church."

"Oh." Elizabeth whispered drawing even closer to her mother. Johnny was already there and noticed them walk in. He got up from the seat behind his grandmother and greeted them before his sister passed out from freight.

"She doesn't know I'm here," he whispered. "Isn't this great? Come, I saved two seats for you. This place is packed." Putting his arm firmly on Elizabeth's shoulder he whispered in her ear, "Don't worry big sister, little brother's here and I won't let the boogie man get you." She punched him in his shoulder.

Steven St. John found a seat on the very last row of the church and observed the insanity-he thought- going on.

"What on earth could have brought my wife to this place?" It was beyond explanation. The praise was so high that no one noticed him except Calvin. Steven looked around at all the black faces with trepidation. He had never seen this many in one place at one time. He was mesmerized. Two people not so caught up in all the happenings said to each other, "You see that?"

"Sure do."

As the miracle unfolded he found himself moving closer to the front of the church where he could get a better look at all the commotion. He saw the woman that was getting all of the attention and stood frozen in his tracts. Steven saw Sarah and Rebecca embracing and saw the unmistakable resemblance. Sarah was a twin to his Rebecca only older and a shade darker. They had the same eyes, the same blonde hair, the same…He turned and ran from the church tears streaming from his eyes. The trip back to Lansing was never-ending and the next week was the longest of his life.

CHAPTER THIRTEEN
"ANNA"

Piercing screams penetrated the quiet night air around the apartment complex in Albany, GA. The muffled blows were barely audible to the neighbors. Blood covered the walls and floor of the small room where the carnage was taking place and the small frail body lay in the middle of a large pillow in a fetal position, a white folded cane over her head as if it were a shield. And then there was silence! Around the body lay shards of glass, ripped clothing and a broken knife blade. The body was already turning blue and had begun to get cold.

Anna knew she heard sounds coming from the living room but no one seemed to be there. She had been thinking of the day she and Trahn had planned. Why was he playing games with her? There, there it was again! She heard the rustling of shoes walking across the carpet.

"Is anyone there?" She asked for the second time. Still, no answer. She picked up the phone that sat by their bed and dialed her mother's number. There was no answer! Again she heard a sound! Anna picked up her cane and moved towards the living room. The last thing she remembered was feeling herself fall as she tripped over the pillow.

Trahn Van Nuyen closed the front door to his apartment and left what remained of his young girlfriend Anna Lancaster lying in the middle of his living room floor. It took several moments for his mind to digest the scene that lay before him. He wanted to see if she were really dead but his criminal mind told him to get as far away from this place as possible.

Without a backwards glance, Trahn pulled the door closed, locked the dead-bolt lock and walked away. He heard police sirens blaring in the background getting closer and closer to where he stood. His mind was racing wondering what should be his next move. He took his cell phone and called the number Kim had given him. There was no answer. Once again he found himself with nothing, just like in Vietnam. Everything he owned was in that apartment, all of his immigration papers, his clothing and, most of all, that black folder. He thought of Sarah's Place and went there immediately. He felt Mr. Smith would help him find out what happened to Anna. His mind was in an uproar. He felt groggy unable to focus. In an instant all of his plans and dreams went up in smoke before his eyes. He felt lost. And where was his 'Pops'? "What am I going to tell Calvin?" He asked Sam Smith as he sat shaking before him.

Sam noticed that he hadn't mentioned Anna once. After telling him the story, all he seemed to care about was his own well-being. It took all the will power Sam could muster not to hit him in the face. He wanted him to get out; he wanted to call Anna's mother; and he wished he had never laid eyes on Trahn. "Could Anna really be dead?"

Since Calvin and Sarah left the school, Sam had seen very little of Trahn except when he came to pick up Anna from school. He felt so badly for what Trahn had just relayed to him and didn't want to believe him, but he saw the fear in his eyes and knew that something disastrous had occurred.

"I don't know what happened," Trahn kept repeating. "I woke up and she was laying there and there was blood. I just got out of there."

"What do you want me to do about this?" He asked Trahn. "I can call the police for you if that's what you want; that would be the wise thing to do."

"But-but-but", he stuttered, "they'll think I did it!"

"Did you?" Sam asked looking directly into his eyes. "I don't know," Trahn whispered.

"No!" Trahn screamed, jumping up from his seat. "I loved her." He whispered.

"Then why are you so frightened?" Sam asked.

"There is other stuff." Trahn muttered. There are things in my apartment that the police might frown upon and not understand. I can't explain right now, but I didn't kill her, I swear." Sam didn't believe him.

"Can you go to my apartment and get something for me, Sam? I heard sirens as I left so someone must have already called them."

"Sorry, I can't do that. What is so important that you can't get it when all this is over?"

"I can't tell you right now, Sam, you have to trust me."

"Trust you…..? Sam scratched his head.

It was 5:30 p.m. and all of the students had left the school for the day. Trahn looked around at the familiar sights and groaned. He made his way to the Chapel in Sarah's Place and fell to his knees begging his God to help him out of this situation. "Lord, I know you don't know me but my name is Trahn and I need help. Can you hear me, Lord?" Sam Smith picked up his phone.

CHAPTER FOURTEEN
"CRISIS"

For two days the Logan household was aglow with wonder and thankfulness. When Sarah saw her daughter's face again after so long a time she was once again amazed at how much they looked alike, but she also saw Mr. Lawrence in her and wondered briefly what had become of him. It was just a fleeting thought. She would let nothing spoil this glorious time for her and Calvin.

Newport was buzzing about the miracle and once again Sarah Elaine Justin-Hansen-Logan was the talk of the town, an anomaly. Full circle!! Rebecca and Elizabeth stayed a week and Sarah shared with them as far back in her life as she could remember, leaving nothing out. It was like a cleansing took place for all of them. She was in total awe of God's love and mercy. In the midst of all of the joy, however, she could see that Rebecca was troubled and she wondered what she could do to help, but Rebecca never broached the subject and Calvin didn't mention the man that had followed her into the church that day.

When the time came, Rebecca was reluctant to leave her mother but Elizabeth needed to get back to whatever it was that she did, Rebecca really didn't want to know. She was in graduate school at the University of Michigan, Detroit branch, and what she was majoring in changed monthly. Johnny was a successful car dealer in the city and was following in his father's path. He was carefree, unattached and very happy. She loved them both and cherished the time they spent together.

The drive from Detroit gave her time to reflect on the events of the past month and her mood had indeed shifted. She was now fully prepared to tell Steven about her past and the rest of the family that she had neglected to talk about but, when she opened the door to their home there was silence and she knew he was not there. Somehow she knew he was gone. There was a note on the vestibule table that said in bold print; "WE NEED TO TALK!! Steven.

She woke in a cold sweat, frightened by the reoccurring dream, but this time when she reached for Steven, his side of the bed was empty. She sat up startled and looked about the room calling his name. There was no answer. She looked at the bedside clock and the time was 5:30 a.m. She knew he hadn't been home last night when she returned and there had been no phone call. He didn't return the page she sent upon her return. He often worked late so that didn't disturb her, but now she was beginning to worry.

It was not like him to stay away from home. It was his pride and joy and he loved being there entertaining his friends and showing off his success. She would see him in a few hours at the courthouse. She returned to bed for two more hours of sleep. Court began at 9:00 a.m. She arrived at about 8:30 a.m. and headed straight to Steven's office.

Steven's chambers looked as though someone had slept there for a whole week and they had. In his distress he'd sought refuge in the only place where he felt in full control. There were food take-out boxes thrown about, soiled clothing on the sofa, and papers piled three deep on his mahogany desk. He had not shaved for days.

"Have you been conducting court looking like that?" Rebecca asked as she entered the room walking to him to give him a kiss. He pulled away and said, "What do you care. You lied to me, Sarah! He screamed at her as his face turned crimson red. Instinctively, she knew. Now was the time, today was the day. Lay it all out, Girl! She wouldn't argue with him for she felt that she had been wrong. She wondered what had happened to that fun-loving man she'd married.

Rebecca picked up the phone on the desk and called both courtrooms, his and hers, and told the bailiffs that they would have to get someone else to replace both of them; that they were having a crisis and couldn't be disturbed for a while.

"What a drama queen." One bailiff said to the other.

They began to talk and five hours later they both sat there staring into each other's eyes wondering where they would go from here. They felt like total strangers meeting for the first time. Nothing was spared, feeling were mangled, myths debunked and truths told. He walked from the courthouse, got into his car and drove to the nearest hotel. She stumbled to her car, tears blinding her swollen eyes, and headed for home drained of every ounce of strength she had left.

PART III

CHAPTER FIFTEEN

"I can't do it." Calvin said. "He's my son."

"She was also your student," Sam countered. "Where is your reasoning man? Don't you think she deserves a decent send off? You know she didn't have a church she could go to other than the chapel. Anna's whole life was wrapped up in this school. We are her family. I never figured you for a coward."

"I don't know where the conflict is coming from. I can't change what happened. Trahn will have a fair trial and if he's not guilty for her death; it certainly seems he's not innocent on all of the charges brought against him, by his own admission; then I would have deprived Anna of having the send-off she wanted. But what if he's guilty? It seems so hypocritical for me to stand there and eulogize her without mentioning that I am her killer's adoptive father. Don't know if I could deal with that."

"Yea, when you put it that way... Sam empathized with his friend. "Anyhow, the facilities are yours whenever you need them."

One week later, Anna Marie Jorgenson was laid to rest without the presence of the man she had sworn to love for the rest of her life. There was no way the authorities were going to let him out of jail to attend a memorial service for the woman he was charged with killing.

Barbara was inconsolable and no one tried to say anything of comfort. What do you say to a woman who has to bury her only child? Sarah Logan sat just as comfortless while she watched her husband struggle to get through the details of a life that ended way too soon. She looked around at all the faces she had longed to see while teaching these people to sing, play instruments and regain some of what they had lost by being blind. Anna had missed their last performance because she had chosen to run off with Trahn. Oh, if only she had made a different choice. Sarah grieved because she felt she should have spent more time with the 22-year old young woman and supplied more guidance, but would that have made any difference?

Sarah shook her reverie and listened again to her husband. She prayed that he wouldn't dissolve in tears. Her prayer was answered. Calvin's thoughts were back at another funeral where he was responsible for burying another woman that was gone far too soon and he had no power or will to save her. His wife Diana had been found dead on the streets of Norfolk, Virginia from alcohol poisoning. He felt responsible for that death too. Would death and destruction always be a part of his life? "I'm a man of the cloth, this has to stop some time. God, this has to stop."

The city of Albany was outraged at the death of Anna. While its citizens had come a long way from the prejudices of the past, they did not take kindly to a foreigner coming to town and taking the life of a young girl. There was tension between the Vietnamese community and the rest of the city. Once again everyone made their own decisions about Trahn's guilt or innocence and the red flames that illuminated the night sky were not soon doused and the Vietnamese Resource Center burned to the ground.

No investigation was made and the blame was placed on the people it served. "Good riddance, it should never have been here in the first place," was the majority opinion of the city. Trahn looked from his jail cell's tiny window, located in the heart of downtown, and saw the commotion from the demonstration that was taking place. He observed the signs that read, "Go home Chink; no squirrel eaters allowed" to "Baby killer." He was terrified and felt helpless. *I've got to get out of here or they will kill me.* He pondered. He went to the pay phone inmates were allowed to use and placed a call to Calvin. His hands shook as he dialed the number.

Rebecca St. John had resigned her position with the Circuit Court. It was too difficult to return to the bench now that she and Steven had agreed to separate. They had not spoken in months not even when their paths crossed at the courthouse. It was obvious to everyone that something was very wrong.

Rebecca suffered through the trial of her assailant alone, getting her spirits lifted when he was given a long jail sentence assuring that he wouldn't and couldn't do this to anyone else for a very long time. She came to terms with the fact that it was nothing she did while conducting his trial that made him come after her. It could have been any judge who happened to be on the bench that particular day. It was nothing personal. Sometimes desperate people did desperate things.

The irony is, from the circumstantial evidence presented by the prosecution so far in the fraud case, she might have found him not guilty. The defense had discounted most of the testimony presented. Had the defendant let the case run its course, he might have been a free man.

She missed Steven very much but her pride kept her from expressing this to him although he wouldn't return the numerous phone calls she placed to him anyway. At this moment she had no idea where he was living. She realized this dilemma would take some time to work itself out. Feeling like everything she knew about this person was a total lie, wallowing in her misery, was of great comfort. Pity parties had become her specialty and she wore it like a badge of honor.

Clutter surrounded her as she sat aimlessly in her extensive library. Steven still had not asked her to leave their lavish home. When the phone rang, half of her wanted it to be Steven and half of her didn't, Rebecca didn't have the energy for a confrontation.

She recognized her mother's number and hesitated briefly. "Oh, not now Mother," she thought picking up the receiver.

"Hello Mother."

"We need you Rebecca. Trahn needs you. We don't know what to do." All this was said within a fraction of a second and Rebecca had no time to respond.

"Whooo! Slow down. What are you saying? Why do you all need me?"

For the next hour Rebecca listened to her mother recite what had transpired in Albany, Georgia and listened while she begged Rebecca to represent Trahn for Calvin's sake; how they didn't have much money but would pay her as they could. How they had returned to Albany for the duration, however long it took to free Trahn, never mentioning her doubts about his innocence. Sarah was almost breathless by the time she finished her plea.

"I'll see what I can do." Hanging up the phone she immediately sent Steven a text message informing him that he should get someone to close up the house because she was going to Georgia for an extended period of time. Rebecca was hoping that this would get a response from Steven, longing to show him the tremendous sacrifice she was about to make. Sitting in a little apartment only a mile from the house on Maxwell Lane, Steven

St. John smiled and erased the message.

CHAPTER SIXTEEN
"KIM"

The murder case against Trahn Van Nuyen was beginning to unravel. The police had no witnesses and they couldn't disprove Trahn's story of how he found Anna's body. However, they had a live body and were not going to turn him loose until they had another; besides he was to be tried anyway for helping steal the money from the government. Either way, Trahn was not going to be released for a very long time for his own safety.

Witnesses had come forward that tried to establish his movements at the time of the murder. The lies were discounted because Trahn had admitted to being present in the apartment but still insisted that he couldn't have done such a thing and that he couldn't remember what happened prior to his finding Anna's lifeless body. Was this possible? He protested so vigorously that the police decided that maybe they should look in another direction. The Vietnamese Resource Center had burned down and they had no more leads and no one seemed to know what happened to the couple that ran the place. Once the contents of the black binder were released to the public, Kim Lý knew that her freedom was in jeopardy.

"What had gone wrong?" Kim wondered from her hiding place outside of Albany. Her husband Pho had returned to Vietnam on some sort of business and she was in this mess alone. What would she tell him when he returned; if he returned. She had not heard a word from her husband since his departure. She wondered if he knew more than she realized. Her plan had been well thought out and she believed foolproof and it would have worked if Trahn had not bought that stupid blind girl into the picture. He'd promised Kim that he would get rid of her soon but he hadn't. The last time she visited him unexpectedly, she was still there and she lost her patience. Something had to be done. She was losing her control over Trahn because of that girl. Her reasoning became warped.

The money they were taking in abruptly stopped because Trahn had decided that he couldn't think of anymore families to create but Kim knew that this was because he was spending all of his time with that girl, taking care of that blind slut. She trembled with anger.

"He made me do it," she rationalized. "I warned him what would happen if she didn't leave. I told him," she screamed at the mirror that showed the terror in her eyes.

She had gone into hiding after the failed attempt to withdraw money from the created account set up by her and Trahn. Kim was told that the account had been frozen and the assets now belonged to the state until a thorough investigation had been conducted. Kim only had a small amount of money in her own real personal account and she knew that wouldn't last her long with her husband out of the country. She felt trapped!

She'd been questioned by the police about her relationship with Trahn and she was sure that they believed her when she told them that it was no more than an employee/employer acquaintance but they had told her to stay where they could speak to her again if necessary. She protested vehemently that she had anything to do with those phony accounts. She blamed it all on Trahn and had cooperated by telling them how he had approached her about the scheme and she had turned him down. How her husband Pho had been the one to hire Trahn; and how he had left the country and left her to fend for herself; however, she garnered no sympathy and she just wanted to go home to Vietnam. Now, because of that girl, she was stuck.

CHAPTER SEVENTEEN

The dream caused her to wake screaming. Kim was not completely heartless. She'd kept telling herself that what had happened to Anna had been a terrible accident gone wrong. She had relived that day over and over again.

She'd gone to Trahn's apartment that morning and waited a few moments then used the key that she has stolen from him and duplicated to let herself into the unit. She hadn't expected Anna to be there. Trahn had assured her that he had sent the girl home. She entered the living room and sat on the sofa when she heard the bedroom door open.

"Trahn?" Anna called. "Is that you? I thought you had gone." Kim saw Trahn exit from the kitchen and was startled when he saw her. Seeing Anna standing in the door, he placed his finger to his lips to silence Kim. He silently pulled her to the kitchen and whispered. "What are you doing here? I told you I would call you and that you shouldn't come here again. How did you get in?"

"You told me she was going home." Kim sneered ignoring his question about the key. "You lied to me again. Pho is back in Vietnam and now we can be together. If he doesn't come back, then we can be married like we planned."

"Keep your voice down." Trahn looked around the corner to see if Anna was coming from the bedroom.

"Can I have some coffee," Kim asked as she surreptitiously removed a small packet from her purse.

"Okay," he said, "Just one!" When he turned his back to pour a cup, Kim emptied the contents of the packet into the coffee he had sitting on the table. He sipped it deeply wanting to be rid of her. She watched as his head began to droop.

Kim sat stark still not five feet from where Anna stood. When she got no reply; Kim watched as Anna looked from side to side as though sniffing the air. After a few seconds Anna said, "Who's there? Is there someone in here?" Kim held her breath. Anna then turned toward the bedroom door and walked back in. She had smelled the perfume.

Kim could see her reach for the telephone and the cane that lay on the nightstand next to the bed. That's when Kim decided she would get rid of her once and for all. She was in a rage. The sedative had taken Trahn out and he sat with his head slumped on the kitchen table.

Kim moved a big pillow that they kept propped up against the wall and put it into the middle of the floor. She wanted this to block Anna's path when she came back into the room. When Anna walked into the living room, Kim spoke to her. "You're still here I see."

She watched Anna jump with fear and stumble over the pillow Kim had placed in her path.

"What are you doing in here? How did you get in?" Anna screamed. "Trahn, where are you? You should leave."

"You're the one that's going to leave", she said as she flung her body on top of the screaming girl. Anna began flailing at the figure with her collapsed cane but she was losing the battle. If Kim moved to one side or the other, she dodged the blows Anna was trying to inflict. All the while Anna was screaming loudly, "Please somebody help me. Trahn, where are you? Help me, help me....? Whenever Anna felt Kim's breath near her face she would lash out and scratch at her. She hit the mark several times. This infuriated Kim and she felt the blood ooze down her cheek. Kim struck the helpless girl over and over again with all the force she could muster but the girl would not stop fighting.

She still couldn't remember where the knife came from. It was just there. Kim had reached into a drawer in the kitchen and retrieved a large butcher knife. She could still feel the thrust of the blade as she plunged it over and over again into Anna's body. When she came to herself, Anna lay in a pool of blood and only the broken handle of the knife remained in Kim's hand. The folded cane, spattered with blood, was still clutched firmly in Anna's hand. Kim then pulled open the door, shut it firmly until she heard it lock, walked across the street to her car; her clothing soaked with Anna's and her own blood, and drove home. She knew Anna was dead. She remembered how still she was. She had not meant to do that. She just wanted her to leave. Now Trahn belonged only to her!!

"It's all her fault." Kim finally fell into a deep sleep knowing that her life would never be the same and her schemes and plans had failed. She just wanted to go home to Vietnam and never see America again.

CHAPTER EIGHTEEN
"THE TRIAL"

It took Rebecca St. John a month to go through the transcript of the hearing conducted to charge Trahn with murder. She could see how weak the evidence was and tittered when she thought, "In Michigan, this case would never go to trial. Trahn couldn't remember and he had no reason to kill the girl he loved but if not Trahn, then who? There had to be more! Of course his petty crimes, although he had done no jail time, had caught the attention of police and his name came up a few times in some 'pay for protection' cases. These things were also troubling for Rebecca. The way Sarah felt about Trahn had the most effect on the way she conducted her investigation. She was looking for evidence to prove his guilt, but somehow her interviews with him had convinced her that maybe he was telling the truth.

Rebecca knew that Trahn himself was the key to all of the questions she had. Their talks were long and tedious and it was hard to get him to open up to her about his life of crime. He spoke of Pho Lý with great respect and told her that he admired what he was doing for his people here in America. When it came time to talk about Kim, however, his whole demeanor changed and he no longer looked Rebecca directly in the eye. "What is it about Kim Lý that you're not telling me?" Rebecca watched his reaction and was sure he was hiding something.

"I don't know why she hasn't come to see me. She can tell them that I had nothing to do with her scheme. I only did what she asked me to do because, at one time, I liked her a little bit."

"Aha!" Rebecca thought. "That's it. They had an affair! Either she was in love with you or vice versa. Now things make sense." She didn't tell him that the authorities had already spoken to Kim Lý and that she had placed the blame for the extortion directly on Trahn. As far as the detectives knew, Kim didn't even know Anna.

"Trahn," she began, "If I'm going to help you, you have to tell me everything about you and Kim, about your relationship, and about the work you did for the Resource Center. Please don't leave anything out. By the way, no one seems to know the where-a-bouts of Kim Lý. The center is gone and Pho is in Vietnam. So you need to tell me all that you know."

"Gone! Gone where?" He asked.

"It burned to the ground. Nobody seems to know why."

Rebecca sat speechless for more than two hours as Trahn poured out every detail he could remember about his life on the streets of Albany, Georgia. His sincerity was obvious sometimes appearing to be a confused child. But he left out one pertinent fact, that Kim had been present in the apartment that day. He needed to get out of there and find her, then he would get to the bottom of this. Since she was missing he was sure that something had happened to her also. It didn't occur to him that she was capable of such a horrendous act so someone else had to be in that apartment, but who?

"Will I be deported?" Trahn asked her.

"I can't tell you that right now. I just want to get you out of jail. I believe your story."

"Thanks," he said. "You seem to be the only one that does."

"No," she said. "Calvin believes you too!

"Get me out of here and I may be able to find Kim. I know some of the places she used to go to get away. We went there together a lot to keep from running into Pho. I don't know which place she would go to hide but I can try. Just give me a chance. Kim and I have mutual friends and they might talk to me. The Vietnamese community is suspicious of outsiders but they will tell me what the word is on the street."

"I'll make some phone calls." Rebecca said. "Do you know how to pray?" She asked

"No." He said.

"I suggest you learn."

"Well, Judge St. John, isn't it? Your reputation precedes you. What can I do for you?" The judge removed his robe after returning to his chambers from court.

"I hope you got a good report but it's just Attorney St. John now. I resigned my position for personal reasons. Enough said?"

"What do you need?"

"There's a case coming before you. The defendant is Trahn Van Nuyen and I'd like to request a bond hearing. I know the prosecution has a say in this, but I thought I could persuade you to see my side, professional courtesy? He is vital to his own defense. He seems to think this person named Kim Lý can add something but she is missing and he believes he can find her. I think that may be possible." Rebecca flashed a smile. "I would be totally responsible for his appearance in court and even put up the bail. I truly believe that he's innocent of the killing and with his release I believe he can help me track down the real culprit."

"What is he to you?" The judge asked looking for a reaction.

"Long story, Your Honor. When you have time maybe I'll tell you about it, in the meantime; how about it?"

"I'll schedule a hearing for next week but I can't promise the prosecution will go along with this. Isn't this a capital case?"

"How is Monday?" Rebecca asked, realizing that she was pushing her luck, but she pushed on.

"Monday it is," He smiled. "You owe me dinner if I ever find myself in Michigan."

"Deal!" She said raising to shake his hand. "Thank you."

"Don't thank me yet, we'll see what the prosecutor has to say."

CHAPTER NINETEEN

Calvin and Sarah sat in the courtroom as Rebecca made her plea for Trahn's release. They were dumbfounded when the judge set his bail at one million dollars and more astonished when Rebecca offered to cover it for them. Rebecca agreed to put up $100,000 dollars in cash, all of the money she had. Without Steven none of the money meant anything to her. But she also knew that once he went to trial and was found not guilty, she would get the money back. Or maybe not! She felt there was no risk at all. His trial was set for one month from that day.

The wire transfer took a matter of hours and Trahn walked out of the Albany jail a temporarily free man. And Rebecca, Sarah, and Calvin didn't see him again for weeks.

"Have you heard from Trahn?" Was a daily question from all those concerned. Rebecca continued working diligently on the case, interviewing possible witnesses, preparing questions, going over all of the crime scene evidence without any help from Trahn. She was becoming discouraged.

"What if he had run away? What if he had somehow left the country? Why hadn't he called? What if..?" She had no answers, just a lot of faith.

The Vietnamese community was perplexed that their resource center had burned down. There were rumors but no real answers. They had heard about the charges of fraud against Trahn. Some worried that the money they received might be taken back and the government would hold them responsible. Pho had left the country and no one seemed to know where Kim Lý was. When they heard about the charges against Trahn, he was ostracized. The women were the work force in their culture and killing a woman was frowned upon. No one would talk to Trahn so information on Kim was not forthcoming. He visited some of the places they had gone together but nothing panned out. He was getting desperate when he thought of one last place.

They had often visited a cabin nestled in the hills and woods surrounding Albany. Kim had purchased the site with some of the money they had stashed away. They often spent weekends there making love and planning their future away from the eyes of her husband Pho. It was furnished with things that reminded them of Vietnam. Inside was a makeshift pagoda and they sat on the floor on a lavishly decorated oriental rug that was placed strategically in front of a wood burning fireplace where they spent hours massaging their bodies with oil until they came together in hot passion.

"That's it," he thought. "That's where she is." How to get there was his next problem. His car and all of his possessions had been confiscated and he had no money but he had to get there. He went to the restaurant where he had spent so much time and took a chance. He sneaked into the back door of the kitchen one night and cornered one of the dish washers using the intimidation he had used when he collected protection money. One more thing to add to the growing charges against him; he was desperate!

"Give me the keys to your car," he snarled as he eased up behind the man holding a butter knife to the man's back to convince him that he had a gun. "In my left pocket," the man said, not looking to see who this was. He didn't want to know.

"You'll get it back soon." Trahn assured the terrified man.

"What am I doing?" Trahn asked himself as he drove the 50 miles out of the city. He had no choice. If she was there she could tell him what really happened that morning. She was his only chance to prove his innocence. Surely she would tell him what happened to Anna.

The lights were on in the cabin and he looked through the window and saw her lounging on the Oriental rug. When he knocked loudly on the door, he thought she'd be happy to see him. When she opened the door however shock and fear covered her face.

"Wwwhat are you doing here?" Kim stammered. "You're supposed to be in jail."

"Kim, I didn't kill her. You know I didn't do it. Did you put something in my coffee? No one else was there. Why would you do that? You must have drugged me. Did someone else come into the apartment while I was sleep? He grabbed Kim by the shirt she wore and pulled her closer to him.

"Yes, yes, that's it," she said. "Somebody came in trying to rob me and Anna. He kept asking for money. Anna was hitting him with that cane and I somehow escaped." She lied. "We were screaming for you to help us but you were sound asleep." He listened as she wove this fantastic tale about what happened to Anna and he watched as she broke out in a sweat.

"I came up here because after I heard about Anna I was afraid for my life." Kim said.

"So why haven't you come forward to tell the police this story and clear my name? Were you going to let me rot in jail?"

"No," she insisted. "The police talked to me once but I was afraid they were going to ask me about your black binder. How could you be so stupid writing down all that stuff. They have frozen that account and we don't have any way to get the money."

"I know, and you blamed everything on me. Some lover you turned out to be." Trahn watched her reaction. "Did you know Anna was dead when you left her there to fend for herself?"

"Anna!" Kim screamed. "What about me? I could have been killed too. She got in our way Trahn. It's all her fault that all of this has happened. Don't you see that if she hadn't been there, she would be alive today. I warned her! She kept us apart."

He listened as she unraveled and began yelling things that made no sense. He then knew that she had killed his Anna and that everything she had just told him was a lie. Now all that was left was to get her to come back to Albany with him. He knew her psyche was fragile and he had to be careful so that the same fate didn't befall him. He had to somehow convince her that they could retrieve the money and escape to Vietnam. Trahn pulled her into his arms, kissed her deeply, and soon they lay together on the rug holding on for dear life wanting all the drama to go away. He had to convince Kim that he indeed loved her and that they would get through this together and Kim thought that she had gotten away with killing Anna.

"Let's go back to Albany and get the money. Do you still have a passport?" Trahn whispered in Kim's ear after their lovemaking and she lay purring like a kitten. "Maybe we can get someone to impersonate a government official and tell the bank that they need to move the money to another place. Do you think that will work?"

"We could try," Kim responded, knowing that this was all folly. She just wanted to be back in Vietnam with Pho. "If the police don't find the man that tried to rob me and Anna, He will try to kill me if I go back."

"Don't worry, Kim, I'll protect you. Once we get the money, the boys will make sure we get out of the country safe. Just come with me and all this will be over soon and we will be rich just like you told me." Trahn felt sick.

CHAPTER TWENTY

Sarah wanted desperately to go home to Newport. They were cramped and uncomfortable living in the small quarters that Sam graciously provided. She was sorry she'd gotten Rebecca involved in all of this mess and it was driving a wedge between her and Calvin. They hadn't had a conversation that didn't include talk of Trahn's upcoming trial and her nerves were frayed. She rarely saw Rebecca because she was always busy preparing one thing or another. Most of all she missed the church. She knew everything was well, but she wanted to be there. She was convinced that they would never see Trahn again and she was happy about that although she didn't want Rebecca to lose the money she had posted for his bail.

Calvin seldom spoke to her anymore because she refused to discuss how to defend Trahn or how to get him free from the charge of murder. The chest pains were coming more frequently and more painful than in the past. "It's the stress" she convinced herself. "When I get back to Newport I'll go see about it." Rebecca nor Calvin didn't seem to notice her anymore and she felt abandoned.

Sarah began spending long hours at the school again, and to pass away the hours, she began to sing with the students but all they wanted to talk about was Anna. Seeing all the sadness around her made her long for the times she couldn't see the distress on people's faces.

"Ms. St. John, this is Officer Ford from the mid-town precinct. Would it be possible for you and the Logan's to come down here as soon as you can?" Rebecca had made a make-shift office out of her mother's old room at the school and the phone amused her because of all the dots and the like placed on the numbers.

"Can you tell me what this is about?" Rebecca asked. "I'll have to locate the Logan's, but we'll be there as soon as possible. Can you give me a hint?"

"Nah, you all just come on in, now." Rebecca heard something in his voice, a chuckle perhaps? She found Calvin in Sam's office and Sarah in the chapel as usual. They both had that look of dread on both their faces. "Has there been word from Trahn?" Calvin asked. "His trial begins next week and we have no idea where he's at. If he doesn't show for the trial, what are we going to...? Rebecca stopped him and said, "I think the officer would have told me if they had arrested Trahn. Frankly, he sounded as if he had some good news for us or maybe I'm just reading more into the call than I should. Either way, I think it's best if we all go on down there."

When they entered the precinct, Sarah smelled a scent of a perfume in the air. "That's it." She said to Rebecca.

"That's what?" Rebecca asked.

"Do you smell that perfume? That's the same fragrance I smelled in the air when we went to Trahn's apartment right after all of this happened."

"Are you sure?" Rebecca asked.

"Of course I'm sure," her mother whispered. "Remember I had to rely on my other senses for a long time and I have a very keen sense of smell, touch and hearing." she said proudly. "Whoever wears that perfume was in Trahn's apartment. I'm sure of it."

"We'll talk about it later," Rebecca said.

The officer welcomed them at the door and said, "Follow me." They followed him to a small room located in the back of the long corridor. He opened the door and they all gasped when they saw Trahn and an older Vietnamese woman chatting together. Rebecca knew immediately who she was but Calvin and Sarah didn't. Sarah looked at Rebecca when they both smelled the perfume. "That's it," she mouthed.

"Trahn, where have you been?" They all asked simultaneously.

"Around," He smiled. "This is Kim Lý and she has something she wants to tell you."

After telling them the same lie she had told Trahn, Officer Ford asked her if she would submit to a polygraph test. Realizing that she was trapped she looked at Trahn with such hatred it made him recoil. "You never loved me did you?" she hissed. He turned his head from her gaze. When he turned his face away from her, Kim reached over and slapped him so hard that it left the print of her hand on his red and bruised cheek.

"You stupid fool," she hissed. "We could have had everything but nooo, you had to have that little blind hussy. I warned you but you didn't listen. If I can't have you, no one can." She reached again to try and attack him but the officer reached for his handcuffs hanging from his belt. Kim began to scream something in her native tongue over and over again and only Trahn knew what she was saying. His face turned as white as a sheet and tears fell silently from his eyes.

Sitting forlornly before Rebecca and Officer Ford, Kim made a full confession to the murder of Anna, still insisting that it was an accident, and detailed all of the schemes to defraud the United States Government. This was done with two conditions; that she be deported back to Vietnam to serve her jail time and that all charges be dropped against Trahn.

As Officer Ford escorted her, handcuffed, from the room, Kim slowly turned towards Trahn and said, "You ruined my life and I hope you and Anna rot in hell." He prayed she would get the help she desperately needed. Why hadn't he seen this side of her before now? His confidence was shattered, the swagger was gone and Calvin now saw the 10-year old boy that he had bonded with so long ago in the jungles of DaNang.

Six months, 24 days, five hours, and 20 minutes from the day of his arrest, Trahn Van Nuyen walked from the Albany City jail a free man except for a large fine, restitution to the U.S. government and five-years of probation and Rebecca got her money back telling Trahn that this time he was on his own. Most of the next 10 years of his life would be spent paying back all that he owed. Rebecca couldn't wait to hear how Trahn had gotten Kim to come into the precinct with him and pulled this off.

"What did she say in there that affected you so?" Rebecca asked Trahn.

Trahn hesitated for a second and then said, "She cursed me and my family for the next five generations. In Vietnam there are people who can do that sort of thing." But as they walked out the front door he leaned over to her and asked, "Sister, do you know how to pray?"

CHAPTER TWENTY-ONE
"STEVEN & REBECCA"

The Lansing Post's lead story read: "LOCAL JUDGE GIVES UP SEAT TO HELP FREE AN INNOCENT VIETNAMESE IMMAGRANT FROM JAIL IN ALBANY, GEORGIA (Page 3)

Page three: "Local retired Circuit Judge Rebecca St. John goes south to defend the adopted son of her mulatto mother's African American husband in what turned out to be the murder of a young blind girl that he had stashed away in his apartment....Trahn Van Nuyan apparently was brought to America by his Sponsor, the Reverend Calvin Logan, a black well-respected minister with a mega-church, who is the husband of the now revealed "birth mother" of The Honorable Ms. St. John, Sarah Logan. Wow, That's a story within itself. Sounds like the United Nations. It appears that Sarah Logan's birth back in the 40's caused quite a stir in the rural town of Newport, Tennessee because of her parentage, a white father and an African American mother, ooh but I digress. I ask the question; Have the St. John's been living a double life? I'm just askin'!" The article continued.....

Steven St. John's jaw dropped and he choked on the coffee he was drinking. He was in the break room where most of his colleges went for lunch at the courthouse. He saw several of his acquaintances unfolding the paper preparing to read the day's issue. He literally ran into the frame of the door trying to make an escape. This only brought their attention directly to him. Responding to his actions, it was clear that some of them had already read the headlines. Several of the judges looked at Steven, back at the paper, then back at Steven. He thought he would lose his lunch right there on the break room floor. Fear and humiliation paralyzed him. He rushed from the building forgetting that he had an afternoon session.

Once he reached his apartment just blocks from the courthouse, he continued to read the full page ad in the paper which was filled with undertones of racism and innuendo, some even suggesting a relationship between Rebecca and Trahn. "How could they write trash like this and get away with it?" He asked the walls; punching one of them as he walked by.

There had been no communication between the two of them for over eight months and he had wondered where she could be. None of their friends seemed to know where she'd disappeared to and frankly didn't really care. Her phone calls and text messages had suddenly ceased and he was beginning to miss that; even though he hadn't responded to any of her calls.

He needed to think and sort out things in his own mind and had just recently decided that the fault lie with him. There was no great epiphany, no intense revelation, it was just that he loved his wife more than anything and her ethnicity didn't define who she was to him, plus, he missed that sexy body and he wanted her desperately. He dialed her number!

Basking in the glow of her victory Rebecca had decided to languish in her bed all that day after having been away from it for seven months. When the phone rang she debated. "Hullo!" She said slowly. Her eyes were closed and she failed to check her cell phone to see who was calling.

"Hello Gorgeous." The voice on the other end sounded familiar but she didn't recognize it right away.

"Who is this?" Rebecca sat straight up in her bed still experiencing fear.

"Your husband!" Steven said. "Has it been that long?" Both ends of the conversation went silent. There was dead air for about five minutes, neither one knowing what to say to each other. Steven broke the silence. "I need to see you."

"Have you forgotten your way to 5560 Maxwell Lane?"

"No, may I come for dinner?"

"It's your house too Steven."

"Tell Tilly to make something special."

"No, I think I might want to do that myself." Rebecca smiled at the phone. "Besides, Tillie doesn't work here anymore."

"Have you read this morning's newspaper yet?" Steven asked.

"No," Rebecca yawned, "I'm sure it's on the front porch. Why?"

"Don't read it until I get there."

With her curiosity peaked, Rebecca pulled herself from the bed and retrieved the paper and began to read.

"Seems we have no secrets anymore," Rebecca told Steven as he entered their home. They talked about the trial and he told her about the recent information he had gathered regarding his own heritage. They looked into each other's eyes and burst into laughter.

"What a waste of time," he said to her. "All the time we spent on concealing who we really are has made us miss all of these past months together. I found that stupidity has no color." He gathered her into him arms and all the months apart faded into the past. Her special dinner had to go into the freezer for another time because they were both full from their passionate love-making and Rebecca made only one request.

"No more racist jokes?"

"I Promise."

CHAPTER TWENTY-TWO
"BEGINNING OF THE END"

When the new millennium dawned, Sarah Logan found herself on the banks of the Jordan River with thousands of other believers. This had always been a dream, an unattainable dream until now. Thinking of the circumstances that got her there she wondered; was it just luck or was there really something to that Scripture that said, *"Delight thyself also in the Lord; and he shall give you the desires of thine heart? Psalm 37:4.*

So many thoughts raced through her mind as she stood gazing at the murky waters. Somehow she thought the water would be clearer than it appeared. Sarah had envisioned seeing her reflection, and maybe inside her heart, when she looked into the depths of this magical, mystical river, but she had not.

Was it because she stood there beside a man that was not her husband, the person responsible financially for her being there? Or could it be that her daughter and husband, the Pastor, Calvin Logan had no idea where she was at this time? Why was her husband so, so, archaic? What made him think that a woman and a man couldn't be friends without sexual tensions or deeds getting in the way?

The friendship she had with William Moore was precious, unique, rare, invaluable, and at the same time costly. When this pilgrimage was over, would it cost her the marriage she wanted and needed? Had she expected too much and had the past ten years taken its toll? The ordeal with Trahn had drained them both and tested their faith as well as their commitment to each other.

"William, how can I ever repay you for this?" She turned her tear stained face to his. "You have no idea what this means to me."

"No trouble at all." He replied

William Moore and Sister Sarah, as she was affectionately called by the congregation that attended her husband's family oriented, dysfunctional church, had become acquainted when they had taken over the church from his father. The relationship developed without either of them really noticing, but the rest of the congregation didn't miss it.

"Have you noticed that everywhere Sister Sarah goes, William Moore seems to be right behind her?" Sister Vera Mae loved to ask questions like that. Most folks ignored her, those like Pastor Logan, but there were some who supported her every word. He'd heard the gossip but he didn't suspect that Vera Mae might have an ulterior motive, but his heart was grieved when his wife asked to go on the pilgrimage.

The money they'd spent all of those months away from home, living in Albany, helping to defend Trahn, had depleted a lot on their finances and his small salary from the church wouldn't cover what she needed. There was no way he could send her. Calvin had noticed her restlessness since they returned to Newport. The ordeal that just ended had caused division between them. Even with prayer he was at a lost as to what to do. Since the marriage, they had rarely spoken of money so he was not aware of Sarah's financial state and she was not aware of his. All she knew is that if she needed something, it was always there. The savings Calvin had accumulated from his years of military service and government work now came to him in the form of a monthly pension. They shared their earnings from the Blind School and those were now almost diminished. Sarah knew that they were not destitute but that things were getting tight.

Calvin felt badly when he told her, "Sorry, Honey, but there is no way you can go this time. We'll consider it the next time."

"Maybe I could get a part time job to pay for the trip or I could ask Rebecca." Sarah's disappointment showed in her countenance.

"I won't hear of it! That would be out of order. I'm the man of this house and I will be the one to supply the income, food, shelter, and everything else we need. How many times do we have to go over this? End of discussion." Calvin walked from the room.

When considering all the ways she could possibly raise the money for the trip, like a bake sale, a car wash, a raffle, William Moore never came to mind. Had she thought of him, she would never have garnered the courage to ask. This was something she wanted and needed to do on her own.

For weeks she prayed and thought about the trip, but still there was no solution. On one particular Sunday, she woke with a feeling of anticipation and excitement. As she dressed for church, she looked at her reflection in the mirror and swore she saw a glow on her face she had not seen in a long, long time. As she joined Calvin for breakfast he noticed a difference in her.

"Are you feeling okay this morning, Dear? You look flushed. Maybe you should stay home today. The Lord will understand."

She still had not discussed the pains in her chest and the shortness of breath she'd experienced. "I'm just tired," she told herself.

"No, oh no. I don't want to stay home. I feel fine. As a matter of fact," she continued, "I feel fantastic."

The morning Sunday school lesson was spirited. The whole congregation seemed animated and ready for worship. Ms. Snowden and the choir sounded good even though some of them were tone deaf. Was this what her good feeling had been about?

As usual, after Sunday school, some went to the kitchen of the church for a snack before the afternoon service. Sarah's back was turned when she felt him approach her from behind. She was at her normal post serving coffee when she heard his footsteps. Thinking it was Pastor Logan she turned toward him and put on a welcoming smile. She looked into the smiling eyes of William. "Mornin' Sister Sarah," he began.

"Good morning Mr. Moore", she said, blushing a little. Although there was nothing between them, she knew that if she allowed it, their friendship could blossom into something that could be very destructive, immoral and sinful, so she always felt a little uncomfortable in the single man's presence.

"If you have a moment, there is something I'd like to discus with you."

"Of course I have a moment. What is it?" A touch of anxiety filled her heart.

"Have you heard about the trip to the Holy Land?" He began.

"Yes, yes I have."

"I don't mean to be brazen, but I was wondering if you would like to come with me on the pilgrimage as my guest?" I will ask Pastor

Logan's permission if that's alright with you. I don't know why but I felt led to ask you this and to pay for the trip if you want to go. You do so much around here I think you deserve this."

She wondered if he could see how rapidly her heart was beating.

"Oh what a nice thing to say, but I couldn't possibly consider something like that."

"Of course you could. I told you that I needed to make the offer and if there is a blessing in it for me, well, you wouldn't want to stop that would you?"

"Absolutely not," she smiled. "In that case, I'll think about it. Nonetheless, if and when the time comes, I will tell Pastor myself. Thank you for the offer."

"My pleasure, however, you must give me your answer soon because the tour is filling up fast. This is already November and most of the seats will be taken before Christmas."

"Yes, yes, I will. Could she possibly agree to this proposal?

"Absolutely not!" Calvin raised his voice in her direction. "How could you ask such a thing? What would the congregation say? How could you...." Pastor Logan's breath came in a raspy whisper. It was not Sarah's way to be rebellious and he was angrier with his wife than he'd ever been. He didn't understand how she could possibly want to make such a trip without him. Something had come over her he'd never witnessed before and he didn't like it. There was defiance on her face. "We won't talk of this again." He turned away!

Sarah stood glaring at the man she thought she knew. What did she see on his face? Was it jealousy or a spirit of control? Whatever it was, she decided then and there to accept the invitation and make the journey with or without her husband's permission. There was no more discussion about the trip just as her husband had stated. However, when the date approached Sarah Logan was in the number having left her home surreptitiously on the pretense of visiting Rebecca in Lansing.

The tour group stood on the banks of the Jordan River, all dressed in White flowing robes, listening to the minister who stood about 50 feet from the shore. They were all going to be baptized and he was giving them the procedures. Suddenly the skies seemed to open up. The billowy, swollen, puffy clouds just disappeared and in their place was a void with a great bright light that shined directly on the small group. The light was so bright that everyone used their hands, towels, or whatever they had to shield their eyes from the glare. Some started to shake, some started to whisper, "What's going on?" The minister stood transfixed in the middle of the water. It was as if he had turned to stone so still was his body.

Immediately the whole group seemed to understand what was occurring and they all began to pray in unison. It was occurring just as Sarah had envisioned, just the way they all had dreamed it would. As they stood clasping hands firmly, they saw the most glorious sight they could have ever contemplated. There He stood in the middle of the void, surrounded by the light, hands stretched out towards them. "Come!" The word was so faint she barely heard it, but hear it she did. "Come."

Abruptly the minister shouted, "into the water, quickly. All of you get into the water." But it was too late for Sarah. She felt her feet leave the ground where she stood and her body was suspended in midair. She looked down on the others while some tried to grab her feet. She heard William call her name, but she couldn't respond. She didn't want to respond. She felt but didn't see the gentle hand grasp her own shaking hand and pull gently. She heard her own voice cry out, "Will I be saved......?"

Waking from the magnificent dream, her hand reached for the phone on the bedside in the hotel room in Jordan. Her husband's sleepy voice sounded like music to her ears. "Dear, I'm coming home." Tears of joy slid down her cheeks.

"Yes, I know. I'll be waiting for you." Calvin laid back on his pillow and fell into a deep restful sleep!

CHAPTER TWENTY-THREE

Sister Anquenetta Montgomery, as she introduced herself, invaded the front pew of The Temple of the Living God and nothing was ever the same. Pastor Calvin Logan's sermon that Sunday morning was disjointed and not spirit filled; he seemed distracted. Sis. Sassy noticed it right away.

"I sure wish that woman would uncross those big old fat legs of hers and pull her skirt down so Pastor can concentrate." She whispered to no one in particular.

"This looks promisin'," Anquenetta thought. "I have been searching for a church just like this one. Thank you Lord. I like the way the Pastor speaks and look at that bulge in his pants. Oh my, my my." The 40-something year old Anquenetta was what you might call a 'Church fly'; and it flits around from church to church to see where it wants to land for awhile so it can bite somebody. Today she had decided to light in Calvin's sanctuary. The unsuspecting pastor was delighted to see a new face in the pews but somehow he lost his focus and found himself wondering who she was and where she had come from. When the announcement was made for the new visitors to meet with the pastor after service, he found himself hoping that she was the only one.

"Welcome to the Temple Miss ....err?"

"The name is Anquenetta; Anquenetta Montgomery, Pastor," She purred. "I am at your service." She saw the smile crease Calvin's dimpled cheeks and she thought this would be a cake walk.

"I just happened to be passing by this morning and heard that heavenly choir singing and was drawn directly to the door. I knew there was something good to follow. Then I heard you preach and wow..." She flirted shamelessly. The enemy was now at work. Across the table at dinner, he failed to tell Sarah of his meeting as was his routine.

In short order, Anquenetta slithered her way into the inner circle of the Temple and soon became part of the Pastor's Aide committee. Temptation became so thick you could slice it like bread. She was there to serve him water; there to press his robes, there to take his calls; she was just always 'THERE'. Calvin was flattered by all of the sudden attention until one Sunday, Missus Snowden cornered him in his office.

"How you doing Pastor?" She began subtlety. "You and Sis. Sarah alright?" She smiled sweetly.

"Fine, fine, Sis. Snowden. Thanks for asking. Is there something you needed?"

"Yea, it is Pastor. I need for you to stop making an old fool out yourself. You been following that hussy around here like and old dog in heat and everyone is startin' to whisper about it. You too black to blush, but I sees what you are thinking every time she's around." When she took a breath, Calvin interrupted.

"What on earth are you talking about? I know you're not calling my Sarah a hussy are you?"

"You know damn well...Oh Lord, excuse me Pastor. I didn't mean to say that, but you know what and who I'm talking about. Now I know that you're a good man but them are the kind the Devil likes. I thought you were wiser than that. Can't you see what that Anquenetta is trying to do?"

"Oh, is that who you're talking about? No worry, I know who she is and what she is. But don't you think all of God's people deserve a chance to change their ways?"

Missus Snowden pondered that for only a moment and then replied; "Yes, I agree with that, but the Lord don't call everybody and he definitely is not calling her. She is one of the Devil's minions and you best be aware of that. She sashaying around you like a bee to honey. Please don't let her get you, Pastor. Sis. Sarah is all you need. She woman enough for any man and don't you forget that."

That next Sunday Calvin's sermon centered around how Jesus was tempted by the Devil and all the temptations men would experience in his worldly life. He trembled as he thought of how close he had come to being consumed. He sought the eyes of Missus Snowden and winked at her. She knew precisely what he meant. He mouthed to her, "Thank you!"

"I couldn't remember when I thought of another woman in more than a friendly way since I reunited with Sarah, but lately her behavior has caused a strain. I know I have to forgive her but it seems to be a bone of contention for me. Whenever I'm with her, I just think of all the years we spent apart and what we could have accomplished together. I know we would have had beautiful children. If only I could have had a son, just one son, to carry on my bloodline. Was that too much to ask for?

Anquenetta is young and vital and she makes me feel young again. If it worked for Abraham, why not me. She could be a vessel for my son and she is more than willing. Would I be so wrong if I was with her one time? I know once would be enough. But what would I tell Sarah? Stop that foolishness!!"

Time is fleeting like sand running through the fingers of a hand. Convinced that Calvin's crisis, whatever it had been, was over, Sarah Logan's life was settled and the pains in her chest were becoming more worrisome but she kept going building the home she shared with Calvin.

Anquenetta moved on. There was a new ministry in town and she moved on to greener pastures. Sarah purposely went to the church and met the First Lady to include her on her prayer list. Her work at the church became more rewarding as the years passed and all seemed well. The experience she had on the trip to the river Jordan gave her a whole new perspective on her and Calvin's life together. She now understood his disappointment and resentment but she also knew that he loved her as she loved him and trusted him.

Recently Sarah had noticed this person every time she went to church, but had refused to speak to him. He seemed to make his home in the doorway of the office building down the street from the church. While there was no outward evidence of that, he was just always there.

This morning he stood in his usual spot as Sarah headed towards the steps of the building. His clothes contained spots from a month's worth of dirt and grime, the color no longer recognizable. She could see and smell that he had not bathed in ages. His long beard and hair contained spatters of gray but there was something about his eyes. The man's youthful eyes danced and sparkled in his head. Whenever their gazes met, no matter what Sarah was thinking about, or fretting about, it all seemed to somehow disappear from her mind. She was curious about why she felt this way; so today she had decided to ask the man his name and invite him to come into the church. She paused before entering the building, turned to him and said, "Sir, what is your name?"

He responded, "My name is John, and keep therefore and do to them; for this is your wisdom and understanding in the sight of the nations, which shall hear all these statutes and say, 'Surely this great nation is a wise and understanding people...'" Sarah turned and rushed away shaken. "He's crazy," she thought.

While not frightened, this man had unnerved her. She rushed into the church and the Usher thought she was ill, her face was white as a sheet and her hands shook.

"What's wrong, First Lady? Did you see a ghost?"

"That man," Sarah whispered. "I finally spoke to that man that sleeps in the doorway of the building over there," she pointed.

"What man is that?" The usher inquired. I have never seen a man sleep in the doorway. Be reasonable, Ma'am, can you imagine what the owner of that building would do if he found someone sleeping in the doorway? He must have just been standing there. Anyway, what about him?"

"That's not true!" Sarah screamed. You must have seen him. He's there every time I come to church, not just on Sunday either. He's been there for months. Someone else must have seen him."

"Well I certainly haven't seen such a person." The usher wondered if Sarah was putting him on, but the look on her face convinced him that she was indeed upset about something. But he didn't know anything about a man.

The rest of the day became more confusing. Sarah began to ask the other parishioners about the man she had encountered but no one acknowledged having seen the man today or any other day.

"He was there I tell you", she said sitting in Calvin's office. "Why would I make up such a thing?" After speaking to Calvin, Sarah began to doubt if she had truly seen this person at all but his words echoed in her mind repeatedly. In the past she had heard about people that imagined things and tried to convince others that what they said was true, but that didn't apply to her at all. "What did they call it?" She asked. "Schizophrenia?"

That evening at home Sarah decided to draw a picture of the man she saw and show it to Calvin. But when she tried to draw and define his eyes something hindered the pen she held.. It felt as if some force controlled her hand. She looked around the room to see if Calvin had entered. No one was there! An idea formed in her mind. Reluctantly she picked up the phone and dialed the usher's number.

"Hello?" Brad's voice sounded like he was either sleeping or distracted in some way. Sarah cupped the phone hoping Calvin wouldn't hear the conversation.

"Hello Brad, this is Sarah Logan. Have you got a minute to talk? I have a plan." He was the usher who had listened to her talk about the man.

"A plan for what?" He answered sleepily.

"It's something that will prove to you that I didn't make up the story about the man." Sarah felt her body tense just thinking about him

"Okay, what's the plan?" Brad said trying to humor her.

"This Sunday you are going to pick me up and take me to church. We will be together and you can see him for yourself."

"Alright but I think you're making far too much out of this. Do you know that it's after midnight? Don't you ever sleep? Where is Pastor at on this?"

"I haven't told him much about it. I don't want to bother him with it right now. Will you keep my confidence? I'm sorry to bother you with this but thank you and good night."

"Don't you mean good morning?" He said as he looked at the now silent phone receiver. Sarah slept fitfully that night and got up from the bed several times not wanting to disturb Calvin's sleep. Again she had the recurring dream that haunted her sleep night after night.

As she requested, Brad picked her up for church on Sunday and as they walked towards the church Sarah asked, "Don't you see him?" Brad simply took her by the arm and steered her to the front door not wanting to tell her that he had seen nothing at all. He had seen no man there!

CHAPTER TWENTY-FOUR

The letter came to the church. Calvin immediately recognized the hand writing of Sam Smith and the address of the School for the Blind in Albany, Georgia. He tore into the letter anxious to hear some news from Sam. They stayed in pretty constant contact and he was a good source of conversation for Calvin.

The ministry was a lonely place at times. There was not much outlet for Calvin as far as conversation or just venting about things that troubled him. He spent countless hours talking to God but he longed for one human he could trust enough to share his thoughts and dreams with.

"What have I really done with my life? Why do I feel so isolated? Where will this ministry be in 10 years? Will I be here in ten years? Does Sarah really love me or is she trying to make up for breaking my heart all those years ago? Have I really forgiven her..?" These questions he posed to God daily in his prayers.

He was deeply troubled by Sarah's behavior lately and there was no one he could confide in or have a discussion with. He felt there was something wrong but she wouldn't confide in him anything about her feelings. Since the incident with 'the man', which no one ever saw, she had become withdrawn and sullen. She seemed to be afraid to go to church alone anymore especially on Wednesday night. At least, currently, she had ceased to talk about him. It was still a mystery.

Sam's letter was requesting that Calvin and Sarah come to Albany again for a reunion of the class that she and Calvin had taught and he wanted Sarah to sing with the chorus one last time. Calvin was delighted. He thought that would be a great way to get her away and cheer her spirits. Their advancing age had stopped some of the travel and Trahn had moved to Newport to be closer to Calvin. He was a changed man. Gone was the cockiness he'd exhibited for so long. Once his probation was over, he was free to leave Georgia. He was close enough to Calvin and Sarah that they had become more dependent on him than ever before.

The day he looked from the pulpit and saw Trahn walk into the service with his wife, a beautiful red headed Georgia girl and his black haired son, was a great moment in Calvin's life. "Is anything too hard for God?" He asked the congregation which deviated from anything he had said in his sermon. On the Sunday that Trahn made his way to the altar during "Altar Call" nobody could contain Elder Logan. His feet shuffled across the floor of the pulpit like a 30-year-old. Only Sarah knew the joy he was experiencing and she beamed with pride.

"His mind is gone," said Ms. Snowden's daughter who now conducted the young people's choir.

"Of course we'll come," his response began as he spoke to Sam on the phone. "Just give us the date and time. Sarah and I need a vacation and this would be a perfect time to get away. Just send the details and I'm accepting for the both of us. She's going through something and she's not communicating very well with me, maybe you can get some answers from her. Thanks for the invitation and we'll see you soon."

Calvin watched Sarah's expression when he shared the news with her. She was delighted and the next week was full of activity and excitement for her as they prepared for their trip to Albany. He was happy when she rushed to his side and threw her now frail arms about his neck and kissed him deeply. "Oh, if I were ten years younger, you would be in big trouble." Calvin smiled at her as he gently rubbed her bottom through the dress she wore. He hadn't seen her blush in years.

"Right, big talker," she said teasing him. Suddenly she felt so much love in her heart that she just wanted him to hold her. She caressed his face and kissed him tenderly, rubbing her fingers across his lips while she moved his hands to her breast. Right there in his office, in the church, on the small sofa there, Calvin and Sarah made love like it was their first time together. His dark skin glistened in the light of day and Sarah moaned in delight as they tasted and explored every inch of themselves. Spent, he said, "Oh, I forgot to lock the door." She punched him in his shoulder realizing that he was teasing her again.

A hush fell over the audience as Sarah Logan walked onto the stage that had been erected in the chapel of 'Sarah's Place.' She was surrounded by the current students along with a stage full of guide dogs. She hadn't realized how beautiful they were. Sarah's arms and legs trembled. Sam, Calvin and Trahn watched with delight. The small band behind her struck up a note to give her a cue.

Sarah Logan stood at center stage. The pink spotlight cast an eerie glow about her silver hair and face. Pink was not her best color. "Those idiots; Why can't they remember that?" She cast her eyes upward to where she knew the lighting crew sat watching her. Silently she cursed every one of them.

Smoothing down the front of the purple sequined dress she wore, Sarah waited for her cue. As the music director Miles Anderson raised his arms, the first pain ripped through her heart. She clutched her chest and bent over to catch the breath she desperately needed. She cast her eyes in her husband's direction and he saw the pleading look. He immediately jumped from his seat and headed toward the stage.

"Hold on Sarah," he yelled. "I'm here." Dramatically her small body slipped to the stage floor while the first row of the audience leaned forward in their chairs not knowing what to make of this. What was happening? "Oh she's just overcome by those hot lights" someone whispered and then the applause began.

Miles Anderson dropped his arms and the small orchestra broke into the first stanza of "Swing Low Sweet Chariot." Looking at Sarah's pale face and glazed eyes he knew this was the end. Slowly the stage curtains began to move as he saw her strain to get to her feet and push the words of the song from her blue lips. She looked behind the stage where the man she knew from the church stood smiling broadly at her, arms outstretched. Suddenly he saw her smile as what appeared to be a tiny puff of smoke drifted upward towards the top of the chapel. Calvin had made his way to the back of the stage and when the curtain was fully closed he rushed to his wife's side, fell to his knees and thanked God for taking her, the love of his life's, spirit to heaven. He had no doubt that is what had just happened.

Sarah heard the music. The words flooded her mind clearly; however, this time she was in a different place at a far different time....

THE END AND A NEW BEGINNING!

EPILOGUE

September 11, 2001, 8:48 A.M. Eastern Standard Time, 5:48 Pacific Time, 6:48 Central; this was a day that Calvin Logan wanted to forget but it haunted his dreams.

He had been very vocal about the event and wanted to use this time to express his thoughts. September 18, 2001, in Newport, Tennessee a new day was dawning and most of the households were turning over in their beds for the second time to throw that annoying alarm clock to the floor where it couldn't disturb the pleasant dreams they were having. The reporter from the Newport Gazette had arrived early for his interview with the pastor of the Temple of the Living God church that was celebrating 60 years of ministry. He was waiting for the 70-year-old Elder Logan to make his appearance. He watched the distinguished looking man walk, with the aide of a cane, into the living room of his home and the interview began. After asking for information and details about the church, the reporter told the pastor that he could talk about anything he chose and he began to speak. The reporter sat listening to him shocked by his subject matter. He began:

"My first remembrance of that day is that I was wondering why there was a persistent knocking on my bedroom door. "Wake up! Wake up!" the voice said. They are bombing New York." I heard the urgency in Trahn's voice, but the sleep that engulfed me had not quite worn off.

The television News Reporters used words like, 'Apocalypse, World War III, human catastrophe,' to describe the disaster that had befallen the cities of New York and Washington, D.C. our nation's capital. The United States of America, the land of the free and the home of the brave, the financial power of the world, the place that was founded on "Love thy neighbor as thy self" had been attacked by terrorist. This horrendous act was foreign to me and it took some moments for me to realize the consequences. Intellectually I knew that four commercial airplanes were hijacked. I know that two of the airplanes were used as weapons to destroy the twin towers of the World Trade Center in New York City, the heart of the financial empire that is America. My mind knows that one of the planes was used to attack the Pentagon, the seat of our military power, in Washington, D.C. and destroyed almost 1/3 of the building. These things I know rationally.

News reporters are telling me that the fourth plane didn't make it to its destined target and crashed somewhere in Pennsylvania, as the brave men on board tried to, (and did) stop the hijackers from taking over the plane at the cost of all the lives on board. I hear the reporters as they begin to announce that over 200 people on board those hijacked planes are dead because the terrorists guided those planes into the buildings described and crashed them along with the souls of thousands of people.

My mind is trying to take in what this television is trying to explain to me. They are speculating that more than (5,000) five thousand lives had been lost in New York alone. That didn't include the ones lost in the airplanes, or the ones lost in the pentagon. Thousands of rescue workers toiled day and night trying to find possible survivors, one week later. They refuse to give up hope. The voices of the fire fighters sound strained as they report that over 300 of their brother firefighters are somewhere lost in the rubble of the brick and mortar that once made up the trade center.

Strong, brave, courageous police offers are reduced to tears as they describe the hope they have for finding over 30 of their own comrades who had come to the rescue of the citizens who were trapped after the first of the two planes hit the first tower of the trade center with the force that shook the sidewalks themselves. One hour later, both the towers collapsed into a heap of rubble, shattering the lives of untold numbers of people in the process.

Three days after the disaster, our President, George W. Bush, called for a national day of mourning and a memorial service which was held at the National Cathedral in Washington, D.C. Only hours after the event, as I turned my television from station to station, I kept hearing people pray. "Let's pray for the families" someone said. "The Congress and the Senate of the Unite States is standing together and calling for a national day of prayer."

"O, God help us in our time of need," they wailed. Suddenly I felt sick to my stomach and I heard myself cry out, "If I hear one more Senator or Congress person praying, I'm going to throw up. Nobody prayed when I lost my Sarah and none of their prayers will bring her back to me. Then I remembered, *Romans 14:11 For it is written, As I live, saith the Lord, every knee shall bow to me, and every tongue shall confess to God.*

Just as it was written, at that moment, it was reported that the whole world was praying for the United States. The question is, "What took us so long?" But somehow the prayers seemed hollow because with the same breath that they prayed with, the President, the congress, the senate, and yes, most of the American people were calling for "Revenge!"

President Bush said, "We want Osama Bin Laden," the suspected leader of the terrorist group, "dead or alive." He continued, "We will hunt them down, and we will make them pay for what they have done to our country." Let us pray!

The television reporters, the political analyst, the brain trust of America began to talk of the men who carried out this contemptible deed. They didn't seem to fully understand how anyone could believe in a cause so strongly that they would give up their lives for it. I heard when they announced that nineteen men had committed suicide for a cause that was so unjust, misguided, deluded, and down-right crazy. To be so passionate about anything is so foreign to us. Our favorite slogan is "What will be, will be. Why sweat it?" According to the reporters these nineteen men had been in this country for years. It seems they were among us, living with us, in Florida, in California, and other places, blending in with us, for a very long time. They were here away from their own countries (it's still not clear exactly what countries they were away from), planning this calamity, all the while knowing that on the day they chose, and the time they chose, they would all die. This kind of logic, or non-logic, is extraneous to us also. One reporter asked the question, "How could they have lived among us all that time and seen how we live, and still be able to carry out such a despicable act?" A powerful question, they asked, "How could this happen?" The ultimate question was on some lips. "How could God allow such a thing to happen to us?"

The young reporter watched as the old man slumped slightly in his chair. "Pastor Logan?" He gently shook Calvin's shoulder thinking he had fallen asleep; then he realized and said to Trahn, "Call 911!"

THE JOURNEY ENDS!

NEWPORT NEWS – September 19, 2001

Local Pastor dies, during this reporter's interview, due to a massive heart attack in his home yesterday morning. By his side was his adopted son Trahn who came to this country with the help of the pastor. He is preceded in death by his wife, Sarah Elaine Logan, who passed away one year ago. Their story is quite remarkable but I don't have the space to tell it all. I have written a portion of my extraordinary interview conducted just yesterday. Services are still pending at this time for the Reverend Calvin Logan pastor of The Temple of the Living God Community Church. Details on page 2. Byline by: Brandon Yoder

Author's note:

Thank you for taking the time to read my latest book. If you have enjoyed it please give me your comments at (alma-bass@comcast.net) Your input is very important to me. God Bless!

CPSIA information can be obtained at www.ICGtesting.com
Printed in the USA
LVOW131330010713

340954LV00002B/5/P